THE MOVING FINGER
WRITES . . .

Crosby laid the cardboard box on the doctor's desk. The pathologist gently raised the lid and reached for his magnifying glass. He peered at the end of the finger containing the fingernail. "If this is anything to go by, Sloan, you've got someone here who took normal care of his appearance."

"The trouble," said Sloan flatly, "is that we haven't anyone here."

"Just the finger," put in Constable Crosby helpfully.

"I shall be very surprised if the rest of this chap here isn't around somewhere," said the doctor.

Sloan took another, longer look in the box. In a matter of moments the pathologist had translated three small bones and a little skin from "Remains thought to be human" into "This chap here."

"Find the rest of him, Sloan," said the doctor cheerfully, "and I'll tell you what killed him."

And then I can find out who killed him, Sloan thought.

Bantam Books by Catherine Aird
Ask your bookseller for the books you have missed

HARM'S WAY
HENRIETTA WHO?
HIS BURIAL TOO
LAST RESPECTS
A LATE PHOENIX
A MOST CONTAGIOUS GAME
PARTING BREATH
PASSING STRANGE
THE RELIGIOUS BODY
SLIGHT MOURNING
SOME DIE ELOQUENT
THE STATELY HOME MURDER

HARM'S WAY

Catherine Aird

BANTAM BOOKS
TORONTO · NEW YORK · LONDON · SYDNEY · AUCKLAND

*This low-priced Bantam Book
has been completely reset in a type face
designed for easy reading, and was printed
from new plates. It contains the complete
text of the original hard-cover edition.*
NOT ONE WORD HAS BEEN OMITTED.

HARM'S WAY

*A Bantam Book / published by arrangement with
Doubleday & Company, Inc.*

PRINTING HISTORY
*Doubleday edition published December 1984
A Detective Book Club Selection, January / February 1985
Bantam edition / August 1985*

The chapter headings are taken from
the office of compline

Bantam Books are published by Bantam Books, Inc. Its trademark, consisting of the words "Bantam Books" and the portrayal of a rooster, is Registered in U.S. Patent and Trademark Office and in other countries. Marca Registrada. Bantam Books, Inc., 666 Fifth Avenue, New York, New York 10103.

PRINTED IN THE UNITED STATES OF AMERICA

O   0 9 8 7 6 5 4 3 2 1

ACKNOWLEDGEMENT

John Imhoff, agricola

ONE

•

Hurt not thy foot against a stone

"There's no barbed wire," said Wendy Lamport, looking along the hedgerow.

"That's something, I suppose," said her companion, Gordon Briggs, grudgingly. He was verging on late middle age and difficult about almost everything.

"And," she said, looking over into the field, "not a bull in sight."

"I should hope not," responded Gordon Briggs roundly. "There's a bylaw about bulls in fields in Calleshire. It's illegal to have a bull more than twelve months old in any field in the county containing a public footpath."

"No warning notices, either, that I can see," carried on the girl, completing her survey of the terrain before them.

"Warning notices," pronounced Briggs pedantically, "have no significance whatsoever in relation to public footpaths and rights of way. You should know that by now, Wendy."

"Yes, Gordon." Wendy Lamport nodded. She had heard him say it time and time again. "It doesn't stop them trying it on, though, does it?" she added.

"Landowners can put what they like on notice-boards," declared Briggs, adding militantly, "but they can't keep us out."

"Let them try, that's all," said Wendy Lamport loyally. "Just let them try."

"That's the spirit," said Gordon Briggs.

It might have been the spirit behind the Berebury Country Footpaths Society but their actual rallying cry was more ambiguous. "Every walk a challenge" was the motto printed under the masthead on their writing paper. The challenge, though, was not usually to the walker. The gauntlet was thrown down in front of the luckless owners of the land over which they proposed to walk. If, that is, those owners of the land happened to have an official public footpath or right of way running over it.

1

"The stile is all right," observed Wendy a little later. "It's just where it says it should be on the map." She was young enough for this fact still to come as a small surprise to her. "Beyond the first turning after the public house."

The Definitive Map, properly marked up, was the society's Bible.

"North-north-west off the Sleden-to-Great Rooden road," said Briggs, who had done his homework.

Barbed wire, untethered bulls and missing stiles were just a few of the obstacles that farmers and other landowners could put in their way.

"See over there," she said, pointing. "There's even a sign saying it's a public footpath."

It was the society's ambition to have all the footpaths in the county of Calleshire signposted.

"It doesn't look," he remarked, "as if we're going to have too many difficulties with the walk proper."

Gordon Briggs did not know it at the time but he had seldom spoken less prophetically.

He and Wendy Lamport constituted a reconnaissance party for the society's next walk, scheduled for the following day. Bitter experience had taught members of the Berebury society that a preliminary survey of the countryside before a group walk saved a lot of frustration. Armed with bill-hook and secateurs the pioneers could make sure that the route was open. Nature's obstructions, though, were as nothing compared with those of man.

"Who's the farmer here?" Briggs asked as they walked forward.

"Name of Mellot," said Wendy Lamport. Feminism might have made some progress but the clerical work of the society was still done by the women. So were the teas. The men, Greek style, sat on the committee and pontificated. She glanced down at her notebook. "George Mellot."

"Any relation?"

"Who to?"

"Mellot's Furnishings, of course." Mellot's Furnishings were a nationwide chain of upholsterers with distinctive purple delivery vans to be seen not only in Calleshire but everywhere in Great Britain.

"I don't know," said Wendy.

"Unusual name."

"Could be the same, I suppose."

Gordon Briggs looked round and sniffed. "No sign of the millionaire touch about this place, although you never can tell with farmers."

"Poor relation, perhaps," suggested Wendy. She had a rich cousin herself and knew what it felt like to be on the less well-off side of the family.

He snorted gently. "Farmers aren't anyone's poor relations these days."

"That's true." They had both seen too many farms in their walks for her to dispute this. Agrarian depressions there might have been in the past—she knew that the turn of the century had been a bad time in Calleshire—but the country certainly wasn't in the grip of one at the moment and this farm looked properly provided with well-kept buildings and good fences.

Gordon Briggs took another look at the map. "And we've just come on to Pencombe Farm now, haven't we?"

"When we turned right off the Great Rooden road," replied Wendy. "That's when Mr. Mellot's land began. The wood we've just come through—"

"It's called Dresham," nodded Briggs, squinting at the Ordnance Survey symbols on the map. "The other side of the road."

"That belongs to someone else," said Wendy. She hadn't enjoyed walking through the wood. In her experience there were woods and woods, and Dresham Wood had had an unfriendly feel to it. There had been a clearly marked footpath all the way through the wood but there had been branches of undergrowth growing across it, and muddy, slippery patches underfoot—to say nothing of the roots of trees laid across the way acting as snares for the unwary.

And a blackbird giving its alarm call.

She consulted her notebook. "Dresham Wood is on Lowercombe Farm. That belongs to a Mr. Sam Bailey." At one moment while they were in the wood she had had the distinct feeling that they were being watched.

Gordon Briggs put his foot down purposefully. "We're still on Footpath Seventy-nine, though, aren't we?"

Walking Footpath Seventy-nine in the Calleshire County Council Schedule was the object of their exercise—in both senses—today. If they found it barred to them by any of the time-honoured obstructions they would follow their society's set procedure. First, a letter would be sent to the landowner,

then a polite visit would be made to him, followed by a
further attempt to walk the footpath, and then—if all else
failed—a letter of complaint would be written to the Calleshire
County Council.

"It seems all right," said Wendy Lamport cautiously.

"We're still near the road," Briggs reminded her.

Long experience had taught members of the society that if
a footpath was going to be obstructed then the obstruction
wouldn't be within sight of the road.

"That's true," said Wendy, adding hopefully, "perhaps it
will be open all the way."

She was a nice girl who didn't relish confrontations with
angry farmers. To be honest she didn't think Gordon Briggs
did either but he was a passionate believer in keeping
footpaths open and if that included confrontation—and it
frequently did—then he would endure that too.

"And it doesn't cross a ploughed field here," said Briggs
significantly.

Wendy Lamport nodded and started to pick her way along
the hedgerow, counting her paces as she did so. Footpaths
that crossed ploughed fields—usually diagonally—were an
especial bone of contention. The farmer found it irritating—
and expensive—to leave the footpath unploughed and offered
the edge of the field as an alternative. Sticklers for accuracy
like Gordon Briggs saw this as the thin end of the wedge....

"Six hundred years," said Wendy suddenly.

"What?"

"This hedge," said Wendy. "There are five different species
of tree growing in thirty yards of it."

"What about it?"

"That means it's six hundred years old, doesn't it?"

Briggs grunted.

"Dendrochronology or something, it's called," said Wendy
inaccurately. She was vague on the figures, too. "They say
you can tell the age of a hedge by the number of varieties of
species growing in it. A hundred and ten years for each
species plus thirty—that's the equation."

"Very likely," muttered Briggs. Unlike a lot of the members of the Berebury Country Footpaths Society, he was
neither a naturalist nor an historian.

Wendy was still looking at the hedge. "Isn't it romantic to
think that that's been there growing like that ever since the
Plantagenets were on the throne?"

"Quarrelsome lot," said Briggs, briefly summarising the Wars of the Roses and more than a hundred years of English history. He had no imagination. He waved an arm. "The house looks old enough to match."

"Where?" asked Wendy. She liked looking at old houses. "Oh, yes, I see."

"That'll be Pencombe Farm, I suppose," said Briggs.

"Isn't it nice?" she said warmly as a substantial brick building came more fully into view. "And how well it nestles into the landscape."

"Pity about the barn," said Briggs.

The girl turned her gaze towards the farm buildings behind the farmhouse. A modern two-ridged barn in precast concrete rose behind the farmhouse, standing out like a sore thumb. Soaring above the farmyard were a handful of crows. "It is a bit—well, utilitarian, isn't it?" she said uncertainly.

Briggs shrugged. "Farmers have got to move with the times like everybody else." Briggs himself was a schoolmaster and hadn't changed his teaching methods in twenty years. "I expect the old barn fell down." He turned his attention back to the footpath. "No problems in this field, anyway. Where does the path go after this?"

"Towards the farmhouse," said Wendy.

Gordon Briggs nodded. Many of the footpaths they walked over were relics of those ways used simply by farm labourers to get to work in times past. If it was illogical that this should result in the world and his wife now being able to tramp over a farmer's field for all time Briggs did not let the thought trouble him too much. To him a footpath—within the meaning of the act—was a footpath and as such it was there to be walked and thus to be kept open for posterity. Its origins—be they ancient ridgeway or a Victorian farm servant's short cut to work—were of no interest to him, any more than were the flora and fauna of the countryside through which the footpaths led him. He was a single-minded man and the only thing which interested him about a footpath was whether or not it was open to the public.

"They'll see us if we follow it to the farmhouse," said Wendy.

"A good thing too," said Briggs robustly. He grinned suddenly. "It'll be good practice for seeing forty of us tomorrow, won't it?"

"Yes, of course," agreed Wendy quickly. All the same she

knew that very few farmers relished the sudden sight of the
entire Footpaths Society picking its way over their fields.
Almost none of them could resist the temptation to come out
and make sure that the walkers didn't stray from the footpath.
As it happened that was one of the things that the farmer
didn't need to worry about. Members of the society were
meticulous about keeping to the authorised footpath. It was
one of their canons. Moreover it was in the Country Code.

The two walkers advanced towards the farm. Besides the
new barn there was an agglomeration of older buildings all
set round a traditional steading, four-square against the wind
and the weather. Well over on their left was the drive to the
farm from the highway and the village of Great Rooden.

"This is the older way," said Wendy, pointing to their path.

"How do you know?" asked Briggs.

"It's shorter," she said. "And it cuts off quite a corner. The
road came later, you can tell."

"Distance doesn't matter with cars," said Briggs with all
the contempt of a determined walker. He could be quite rude
to any motorist who was so misguided as to offer him a lift in
his car. "Just wait until the world runs out of fossil fuel, that's
all. . . ."

It was a prospect that he regarded with selfish equanimity.

"The road's higher than the field, too," said Wendy. "You
can see where they had to build it up a bit."

"Shouldn't wonder if they didn't get a bit of flooding down
here in the wintertime," remarked Briggs, looking at the lay
of the land. "These flat meadows look as if they might have
had water in them."

"They're certainly very lush just now," said the girl. "Mind
you, it is high summer."

It was in fact late June and the Calleshire countryside had
an almost idyllic look about it.

"They've got their hay in," she said.

"I should hope so by now." Suddenly Gordon Briggs stiffened
and changed his tone. "But soft, we are observed."

Wendy looked round. "I can't see anybody. . . . Oh, yes, I
see what you mean."

Standing outside the barn watching their approach was a
tall, sturdily built man with a dog. It was a well-trained dog
and it sat obediently at its master's heel.

"Good afternoon," said Briggs politely.

"Afternoon," responded the man in neutral tones.

"Mr. Mellot?" said the schoolmaster enquiringly. Once upon a time you could tell what a man was by what he wore, but not any longer. This man had on well-worn trousers and an open-necked shirt. His shirt-sleeves were rolled well up and he had obviously been working in the barn. He had about him though an unmistakable air of ownership. "Mr. George Mellot?"

"Yes?"

"We're an advance party from the Berebury Country Footpaths Society," said Gordon Briggs.

"Yes?" The farmer was neither friendly nor unfriendly. He just stood by the barn door and waited.

"We're walking a footpath in preparation for our society's meeting tomorrow," announced Gordon Briggs.

The other man stirred. "You mean you're meeting here? At Pencombe?"

"That's right," said Briggs. "We're going to walk Footpath Seventy-nine on the County Survey. You needn't worry," he added quickly. "We shan't do any damage."

"We always keep to the Country Code," chimed in Wendy eagerly. Mention of the Country Code was meant to reassure farmers. Usually all it succeeded in doing was to puzzle them.

This farmer looked as mystified as all the others did.

"We fasten all gates," said Wendy. "And we don't light fires."

"We keep to the path," said Briggs, "and don't damage fences."

"I'm glad to hear it," said the farmer drily.

"And keep dogs under proper control," said Wendy.

George Mellot glanced down at his own perfectly behaved dog and said, "I'm glad to hear that too."

"There won't be any litter either," went on Wendy anxiously, "and we don't damage wildlife or anything like that."

"I'll hardly know you've been, is that it?" said Mr. Mellot ironically.

"That's right," said Wendy with relief.

"We leave nothing behind but our thanks," said Briggs sententiously.

"I see." He looked at them both. "I take it that you already know the route of Footpath Seventy-nine?"

"It's on the Ordnance Survey Map," said Briggs. There

were some farmers who pretended not to know the route of the footpaths over their land.

"It passes the farmhouse," George Mellot informed him, "and picks up the stream and then goes straight across the valley and out onto the Little Rooden road."

"Footpaths always take the easiest way," said Briggs knowledgeably. "No point in making the going harder than it need be."

"I think," said Mellot quietly, "that you'll find it easy going all right. There's nothing to stop you." He glanced at the tools they were carrying. "You won't need your bill-hook either."

"That's a relief," said Wendy. "I'm no good at cutting my way through undergrowth."

"We keep all the paths clear at Pencombe," said the farmer, adding astringently, "for our sakes as well as yours."

"Quite so," said Briggs fussily. "It's good farming practice."

"It makes it easier for the boys to come in and steal my apples too," said the farmer. "Had you thought about that?"

"That's something quite different," said Briggs firmly. "That's a police matter. Don't worry, Mr. Mellot," he added, "none of our people will take anything."

"Except photographs," said Wendy Lamport brightly.

"Very well." The farmer nodded and abruptly turned back into the barn, his dog still at his heel.

"That's all right then, isn't it?" said Wendy, turning to her companion. "We should have a good walk tomorrow."

"We should," agreed Gordon Briggs. "This way, I think."

They passed the farmhouse in its comfortable setting at the bottom of the combe and picked their way along the footpath which followed a stream. The farmer had been quite right. The way was clear; indeed it looked as if it had been attended to fairly recently. Walking along it was quite pleasant and their pace unconsciously quickened. That was when they began to realise that the day was already warm and getting warmer.

Presently Briggs looked at the map again. "Surely this stream is part of the river Westerbrook that finishes up the Calle somewhere?"

Wendy nodded. "Woe waters."

"Pardon?"

"Didn't you know?" she said, surprised. It wasn't often that anyone could tell the omniscient schoolmaster anything. "The

Westerbrook is one of those streams that only flow some of the time."

"They're called intermittent rivers," he informed her in his classroom manner.

"They do say," said Wendy, "that it only flows when something awful is going to happen."

Briggs sniffed. "There's always something to be woeful about."

"If it's flowing," persisted Wendy obstinately, "it presages doom."

"It's more likely," said Briggs prosaically, "that there's a sump under the hill at the head of the valley and when that's full and primed the river starts up again."

Together they regarded the Westerbrook. Its shallow waters glistened in the sunshine.

"I must say it looks harmless enough," said Wendy.

Briggs turned his gaze upwards. "There'll be plenty of water under the hill at the moment. That's why it's flowing."

"We haven't had so much rain lately though," insisted the girl.

"And when it's all emptied away," forecast Briggs, "the Westerbrook will dry up again."

"Woe waters," insisted Wendy obdurately, "that's what they are."

Gordon Briggs shrugged his shoulders and turned away from the stream. The two walkers soon resumed their steady pace, Wendy Lamport in the lead, Gordon Briggs a step or two behind.

That was how it came about that Wendy saw the object first. She had been aware of the crows without particularly remarking on them. There were always crows about on farms and their presence had not especially impinged on her consciousness. Afterwards she could not even remember if she had noticed the actual bird that had flown across the path just ahead of her.

What was certain, though, was that it had dropped something.

Wendy was only a few paces away from that something and she automatically looked down to see what it was.

And for ever afterwards wished that she hadn't.

As she saw what it was that was lying there she halted so abruptly that Gordon Briggs very nearly cannoned into her. He, too, stopped.

"What's the matter?" he asked.

"Look!" whispered Wendy, her face paled.

"Where?" said Briggs.

"There!" She pointed an unsteady finger in the direction of the ground.

"What at?"

"That," she said shakily.

"I can't see anything..." His voice trailed away as he too saw what was lying on the footpath. "Good Lord!"

"A finger," she gulped. "That's what it is, isn't it?"

"It can't be."

"But that's what it is," she repeated, a rising note of hysteria coming into her voice, "isn't it?"

Gordon Briggs nerved himself to bend forward and examine it more closely. "Yes," he said soberly, "I'm very much afraid that it is."

TWO

.

Before the ending of the day

"Remains thought to be human," said Police Superintendent Leeyes more technically.

It was later that same afternoon and he was talking to Detective Inspector C. D. Sloan at Berebury Police Station. Inspector Sloan, who was known as Christopher Dennis to his nearest and dearest, was—for obvious reasons—called "Seedy" by his friends. He was the head of Berebury's Criminal Investigation Department. It was a tiny department but such crime as there was in that corner of Calleshire usually landed up in Detective Inspector Sloan's lap.

"Constable Mason reported them," continued Leeyes.

"Mason from Great Rooden?" said Sloan.

"None other," said Leeyes heavily.

"There's never a lot of trouble out that way, sir," remarked Sloan.

"There's never any trouble at all at Great Rooden," declared Leeyes emphatically. "Ever."

"Not if Ted Mason can help it," agreed Sloan. "You can count on it."

"Mason," pronounced Leeyes flatly, "is one of your anything-for-a-quiet-life type of constables and he sees that there isn't any trouble."

Detective Inspector Sloan knew this too. Police Constable Mason was well known for keeping the quietest beat in the county.

"He grows prize cabbages very well," snapped Leeyes tartly.

"He won't be pleased about human remains then, sir, will he?" said Sloan in an attempt to get back to the matter in hand.

"He isn't."

"Still, sir," went on Sloan, determinedly looking on the bright side, "these remains—they could be archaeological, couldn't they? Perhaps it was an ancient Briton."

"It's not an ancient Briton," said Leeyes, adding sourly, "You're nearly as bad as Mason."

11

"No, sir?"

"It's not an ancient anybody, Sloan," said Leeyes. "There's still some flesh on the bone."

"That's quite different," agreed Sloan quietly.

"It was the flesh that worried Mason, too," grunted Leeyes. "Bones—old bones—you can sweep under the carpet, but not flesh. Not even Constable Edward Mason."

"What's he done about it?"

"Marked the spot," replied Leeyes neatly, "and passed the buck."

"What's he done with the finger?"

"Taken it back home with him," said Leeyes briskly. "At the moment it's sitting in a cardboard box in his office in Great Rooden."

"This farm, sir . . ."

"Pencombe."

"Anything known about it?"

"Never heard of it before," said Leeyes.

"And the farmer?"

"George Mellot," said Leeyes, adding gratuitously, "Nothing known about him either."

"Mason will know him, of course." Sloan was confident of this. What with warble fly and the dipping of sheep and this regulation and that, country constables knew farmers.

"Oh, Mason knows him, all right," said Leeyes. "Mason knows everyone out that way."

"Well?"

"Mason," said Leeyes scornfully, "has reported that George Mellot farms well—which doesn't tell us a lot about flesh and bones on his farm."

"No, sir," agreed Sloan. It told them something about the man though, and that might help. It was too early to tell. "Has he been at Pencombe long?"

"Man and boy," said Leeyes. "Mason knew that much."

"If there's a finger, sir," began Sloan tentatively, "then—"

"I know what you're going to say, Sloan," interrupted Leeyes. "If there's a finger there's usually a body. I know that."

"Usually?" Sloan echoed a word he hadn't expected to hear.

"Not always," said Leeyes testily.

Sloan cast about wildly in his mind. Test tube babies and cloning had come a long way, he knew, but . . .

"There are exceptions," said Leeyes.

"Sir?"

"I never have been entirely happy about Berebury Hospital, Sloan."

"Really, sir?"

"I'm sure if we looked into it that we would find their disposal system pretty haphazard."

"Very probably, sir." The back doors of most institutions were not as imposing as the front.

"They've got to do something with the bits they chop off, haven't they?"

"You think the finger could be surgical waste, do you, sir?" Sloan didn't know if that was what the surgeons called the end product of an amputation, but it would be bound to be dressed up as some ambiguous euphemism. There was nobody better at doing that than the medical profession.

"I don't know," responded Leeyes, "but I do know that we'll look pretty silly in the county if this finger turns out to have come from a man who works in a sawmill who's only got nine left on his hands."

"Quite so, sir. I'll check with the hospital, of course. But if it isn't one of theirs, so to speak, where should we be looking for the rest of the body?"

"Exactly, Sloan, where." On the wall behind Superintendent Leeyes was a vast map of the County of Calleshire. The limits of F Division were outlined by a thick black line. Great Rooden was in the south-east. Detective Inspector Sloan advanced towards the map while Superintendent Leeyes swivelled round in his chair and found a spot with his finger.

"Here's Great Rooden," he said. "Now, where's Pencombe Farm . . . Ah, here it is, Sloan. Just outside Great Rooden on the way to Sleden and Little Rooden."

"Yes, sir." Sloan made a note. Archaeologists had a special word they used for the place where they found bones and other things. It would come to him in a minute. "Right, sir, I've got that," he said aloud. Provenance, that was it.

"It's off the Sleden road if you're going by car."

Detective Inspector Sloan would be going by car. To begin with, anyway. The foot-slogging came later. He said, "These people who found it . . ."

"Two walkers," said Leeyes. "The girl's a bit upset."

"I'm not surprised."

"They were out on a Tewt."

"A what, sir?"

"T.E.W.T.," spelled out Leeyes. "A Tactical Exercise Without Troops." Superintendent Leeyes's time in the army had left him with a distinctly military turn of speech. He enlarged on the theme. "They were prospecting for a walk tomorrow with a group."

"So they were there by accident," deduced Sloan. "Nobody knew they would be coming."

"Not even the crows," said Leeyes.

"I don't know a lot about crows, sir," began Sloan tentatively. Detection made many demands on a man, not all of them foreseeable.

"They eat carrion," Leeyes informed him.

Sloan repressed a slight shudder. It was all very well to use a word like carrion. It was when you came to think about it that it wasn't nice.

"And you know what that means, Sloan, don't you?"

"Yes, sir." He cleared this throat. "If this finger didn't come from the hospital..."

"Yes?"

"Then ten to one there's the rest of the body about somewhere."

"I wondered when you were going to get round to that, Sloan."

"We'll have to find it."

"You will," said Leeyes. "Can't have an inquest on a finger, can we? The coroner wouldn't like that."

"No, sir."

"Besides," said Leeyes, "we'd be the laughing-stock of the force."

"Yes, sir." Sloan could see that that factor took an even higher priority.

"And the sooner the better."

"Yes, sir." That went for all detection. Cold trails made work more difficult.

"And the only man I can spare today," said Leeyes by way of a Parthian shot, "is Detective Constable Crosby. I know you won't like it, Sloan, but you'll have to take him."

"Thank you," murmured Wendy Lamport. "You're very kind." She put her hands gratefully round a proffered cup of tea. Even though it was a warm day she was still shivering slightly.

"You'll feel better when you've drunk it," forecast the woman whom she took to be Mrs. Mellot.

Wendy Lamport and Gordon Briggs were sitting in the farmhouse kitchen at Pencombe. It was a big room with a low ceiling and a great stove at one end. In the middle of the room was the largest kitchen table that Wendy had ever seen. Mrs. Mellot's first reaction to the news about the finger had been to put the kettle on the stove.

"I never have liked crows," she said.

"Nasty brutes," agreed Wendy, shuddering. She put her cup down on the big table. It was made of elmwood, scrubbed white for generations.

"Never mind," said Mrs. Mellot. "Mr. Mason has taken it away now."

"That won't be the end of it," said Gordon Briggs with a short laugh. He exchanged significant glances with George Mellot and said to him, "Will it?"

"Only the beginning, I'm afraid," agreed the farmer. "It must have come from somewhere."

"I said that the Westerbrook only flowed when something was wrong," insisted Wendy tightly.

"Somewhere near," said Gordon Briggs implacably.

All George Mellot's responses seemed to be temperate. "Not too far afield," he said.

Briggs swept on. "The crow would be looking for a quiet spot to—"

"Don't!" implored Wendy. "It doesn't bear thinking about, what it was going to do next."

"You've got to face facts," said the schoolmaster uncompromisingly.

George Mellot, quiet and controlled at the edge of the room, nodded.

"It might have come from somewhere else, mightn't it?" said the girl tremulously.

Mrs. Mellot said quickly, "Of course."

"I mean," she said, "crows fly quite a long way, don't they?"

"Not with something in their beaks," pointed out Gordon Briggs.

"That's what our policeman said," murmured the farmer.

"That means then," carried on Wendy uncertainly, "that you've got a dead body on the farm somewhere."

The farmer seemed anxious not to catch his wife's eye. "I'm afraid it does."

"And what will you have to do about it?" the girl asked.

"Look for it," said George Mellot. "The question is where to begin. . . ."

They were interrupted by a knock at the back door. Mrs. Mellot went across the kitchen to answer it, saying over her shoulder, "that'll be Leonard Hodge."

"My bailiff," said George Mellot.

"I sent a message down," his wife said. "Hullo, Len, it is you, then."

"Come along in, Len," said George Mellot. He explained about the finger to a powerfully built and ruddy-faced man who stood attentively by the kitchen door.

"There's always plenty of crows about at Pencombe, Mr. Mellot," said Len Hodge immediately. He was dressed in working clothes in spite of its being a Saturday afternoon and had the look of someone who had been interrupted at something. There was still grease on his arms, although his hands had obviously been hastily washed.

"I know," said Mellot.

"But I haven't seen no body," said Hodge, shaking his head.

"Have you noticed more crows than usual?"

"Can't say that I have, Mr. Mellot." Hodge looked round at the others in the kitchen and said, "Hard to tell when they're always around. You get used to them being there and don't notice particular like."

George Mellot persisted with his questioning. "You'd have noticed them flocking around anywhere special though, wouldn't you, Len?"

"Daresay I would, Mr. Mellot."

"So would I," said Mellot decisively, "and I certainly haven't."

"Mind you," the bailiff screwed up his eyes, "don't forget that there's upwards of three hundred acres at Pencombe."

"Quite." Mellot nodded.

"And a man can't be everywhere."

"The police will be," forecast George Mellot. "And quite soon."

As he stood up Gordon Briggs ran his fingers over the vast kitchen table and said tactlessly, "They make coffins from elm, too, don't they?"

*   *   *

"A finger?" echoed Detective Constable Crosby.

"That's what I said," repeated Detective Inspector Sloan grimly.

"It's not a lot to go on, sir," said the constable, "is it?"

"It's a beginning," said Sloan. All cases had to begin somewhere.

"But . . ."

Sometimes cases only began with a rumour—a mere whiff of wrongdoing, whispered behind cautious hands. Without anything as tangible as a finger at all. And as often as not they still ended up as full-blown cases too.

"There is nothing to say at this stage, Crosby," said Sloan austerely, "that there is any crime of any sort involved at all."

"Then . . ."

Detective Inspector Sloan climbed into the waiting police car. "It could be just an ordinary death."

"It could be one of those ransom jobs, sir, though, couldn't it?" Detective Constable Crosby clambered more enthusiastically into the driving seat. "You know the sort of thing—pay up or we'll send you an ear or—"

"I know," said Sloan heavily. "Or a finger."

"It's been done before, sir. The Camorra—"

Sloan shook his head. "I don't think so somehow. Not this time. For one thing, it wasn't delivered through the post with a note or anything like that."

"Oh?" Crosby sounded disappointed.

"It was found lying on a footpath."

"Not the same thing at all, sir," agreed Crosby.

"You've been reading too many books," said Sloan briskly. "It's probably just from some old tramp who wandered into the woods to die."

The detective constable engaged gear and steered the car out of the police station. "Where to, sir?"

"Great Rooden."

Crosby grinned. "The real sticks." He did not like the country.

"To the police house first," said Sloan, unmoved. "To see what Constable Mason has to say."

Constable Mason welcomed them to a conspicuously neat house and garden. Mrs. Mason provided tea and homemade scones and a general feeling of homeliness.

"Fancy," she said, "a crow dropping a finger like that. You sit here, Inspector. I think you'll find that chair quite comfortable."

"I'll need to know the names of the farmers on either side of Pencombe too," said Sloan, struggling to introduce a businesslike note into the domestic atmosphere.

"There's Paul Hucham at Uppercombe," said Constable Mason. "He's nearly all sheep. And the Ritchies at Stanestede. That's a mixed farm. Both those farms march alongside Pencombe—to the north-west and east, that is. Oh, and Bailey is at Lowercombe on the other side of the road to the south. Mustn't forget Sam Bailey's land. A road wouldn't mean anything to a crow, would it?"

"I'm surprised that a finger did," said Sloan.

Constable Mason shook a grizzled head. "You'd be astonished what a crow'll take a meal off."

"Another scone, Inspector?" said Mrs. Mason.

Police wives, like doctors' wives, had to get used to mixing life with work.

"You will, Constable, won't you?" she said comfortably, passing the plate.

Crosby didn't need pressing.

"There's no one missing out this way?" enquired Sloan generally.

Mason shook his head. "Not that I've heard," he said. "And I think I would have done."

Sloan did not doubt that Mason's intelligence system was as good as any mechanical one. And his retrieval system a good deal better.

"What about wayfarers?" asked Sloan.

"We do get a few showing up from time to time even in this day and age," said Mason. "If the finger is from one of them we may not know for quite a while. One of the old regulars would have to fail to turn up and that might take months. We might never know."

"It's probably," Sloan repeated his earlier statement, "from some old tramp who wandered into the wood to die."

Constable Mason frowned. "That finger may be from some old tramp right enough, sir, but it's not from a wood."

"Oh?" said Sloan, interested.

Mason shook his head. "Not if a crow had anything to do with it."

There was obviously more to being a country constable than just growing cabbages.

"You won't catch a crow feeding in a wood, sir," carried on

Mason. "They'd be too afraid of being caught by predators for that."

Crosby's head came up from the scones. "Well, well . . ."

"That means—" began Sloan.

"That means, sir," said Mason firmly, "that the rest of this body's probably lying on open ground."

"Should be easy to find then," remarked Crosby indistinctly.

"No," said Mason.

"No?" said Sloan.

"Stands to reason, sir," said Mason, "doesn't it? It's been lying around for a fair old time for it to get into the state it has. I mean to say, fingers don't come off a body all that easily, do they?"

"Another scone, Inspector, or will you have a piece of cake?"

"Thank you," said Sloan.

"So," said Mason, "I should say that it's already been lying around for a bit and nobody's seen it yet."

"It could have just been put out somewhere," suggested Crosby.

"Difficult to move if it's in the state that a crow could pick bits off," said Mason resolutely.

Sloan was inclined to agree with him. A newly dead body was an awkward enough object to move about: A disintegrating one practically impossible.

"Mark my words," said Constable Mason, "that body'll be on open ground wherever it is."

"That should make it easier to find," said Sloan.

In the event he had seldom been more wrong.

"Pass your cup, Inspector," said Mrs. Mason.

"This George Mellot," Sloan said, getting out his notebook, "what can you tell me about him?"

Constable Mason sat back in his chair. "He runs quite a tight ship at Pencombe. Everything done to a high standard and all that."

"What sort of a farm is it?"

"Mixed," said Mason. "Mellot's old man went in for pigs in a big way but you know how it is. Sometimes you do well with pigs and sometimes you don't."

Pigs is equal, thought Sloan to himself. Now who was it who had said that?

Mason carried on. "The place had got a bit run-down by

the time George came to take over. Old man Mellot was a real stick-in-the-mud."

Sloan nodded. Stick-in-the-mud was the opposite of evolution.

"He got like Sam Bailey has got now," said Mason. "Too set in his ways for the good of the farm."

"Wouldn't change with the times," said Sloan. It was easier said than done, changing with the times, especially when those times included incomprehensible technology, computers and microchips with everything.

"There was another thing, sir," said Mason.

"What?"

"Pencombe wasn't big enough for both of them."

"George and his father?"

"George and Tom," said Mason. "Oh, didn't I say? There was a younger brother, too, wanting his share."

Sloan geared himself to hear an updated version of the Parable of the Prodigal Son.

Mason went on speaking. "George bought him out or something and Tom went off to do a Dick Whittington."

It was funny, thought Sloan, that there should only ever have been one Lord Mayor of London to get into the history books. Perhaps it was because he had got into a nursery rhyme too.

"And did he?" enquired Sloan. "Oh . . . ," Sloan answered himself. "You don't mean to say that Tom is that Mellot?"

"Mellot's Furnishings—Upholsterers to the Nation," said Mason neatly.

Not the Prodigal Son then, thought Sloan. More like Joseph . . .

"Best thing that ever happened to young Tom Mellot was being kicked out of the farm," said Mason.

"Some nestlings thrive on being turfed out," said Sloan sagely. Now he came to think of it the name of Mellot had been in the news lately. He couldn't remember the exact connection. He would have to look it up. "Some don't."

All police officers knew that.

"Tom Mellot did," chuckled Mason. "I bet he could buy brother George out a dozen times over now if he had a mind to."

"A piece of cake, Inspector?" Mrs. Mason hadn't neglected her duties as hostess for one moment. "I made it this morning."

He let her finish plying them with food before he asked to

see the finger. Duty, he did know, came first, but there were some things which could wait. Eventually, though, Constable Mason led the way through into his little office and indicated a cardboard box.

"I've got it here," said Mason.

The finger had brought out the atavism that lurks just below the surface in every man. For some reason too deeply primitive to explain in words the constable had laid it on cotton wool.

"It's adult, anyway," said Sloan, taking his first look at it and putting ransomed children out of his mind for good.

"And with a bit of luck," said Mason, "it might just be possible to get some prints off it."

"Too far gone," pronounced Detective Constable Crosby, taking a quick look and stepping back again.

"It would save a lot of time and trouble if it wasn't," said Sloan automatically. Deep down inside himself he knew that nothing was ever likely to be as easy and simple as finding a fingerprint and a person to match it.

"Yes, sir," said Crosby dutifully.

"And now," said Sloan briskly, "we'd better see about mounting a search for the body. Who can we call on out here?"

THREE

•

Brethren, be sober, be vigilant

"This was the exact spot, Inspector," said Wendy Lamport, pointing.

"Right, miss." Detective Inspector Sloan stood on the footpath on Pencombe Farm where the girl had stood earlier. Presently he would get Crosby to take a sample of the grit from the path to compare with any foreign bodies embedded in the skin of the finger. That might help.

"Look," she said, "you can see where the other policeman put that little pile of stones to mark it."

"Yes, miss." Sloan had already noted the infant cairn created by Constable Mason. He looked round about him. "Now, you and Mr. Briggs were walking which way?"

"North-north-west," answered Briggs before Wendy could speak.

"Quite so, sir." Sloan took a quick look at the sun. "So you would have had your backs to the farmhouse?"

"That's right," said Briggs. "We'd come that way, hadn't we?" He turned to George Mellot for confirmation. "You'd just seen us."

The farmer nodded.

"We were heading for the Little Rooden road," put in Wendy.

"And, Miss," continued Sloan, "you've no idea at all in which direction the crow had been flying when it dropped the—er—object?"

She shook her head. "I didn't notice."

"It would save a lot of time," said Sloan, thinking of the area to be searched, "if you had done."

"I'm sorry," she said simply. "You see, we didn't know what it was until after the bird had gone, did we, Gordon?"

Gordon Briggs said, "No."

Sloan turned to George Mellot, who had been standing silently by. He had seldom met a man more continent of speech. "If, sir, you could just show me the lay of the land . . ."

The farmer stirred. "Pencombe Farm runs from the Great Rooden road to the foot of the hill over there. That's where Uppercombe starts."

"That'll be Mr. Hucham's land, won't it?" said Sloan, who had done his homework quite well while he was at Constable Mason's.

Mellot nodded. "And over the other side to the east is—er—Mrs. Ritchie's farm. That's called Stanestede."

"And behind us?" said Sloan, turning round.

"The other side of the road, you mean?" said George Mellot.

"Where the wood is."

"Dresham Wood is Sam's," replied Mellot. "All that land over there belongs to old Sam Bailey. That's Lowercombe Farm."

They were some distance from it but even so Sloan could see a man coming out of the wood. George Mellot saw him too and screwed up his eyes.

"I believe that's Len Hodge, my bailiff," said Mellot. "I told him to start to look around."

"Good," said Sloan vaguely. Crows did not inhabit woods— Ted Mason had said so—but Sloan held his peace. It was no part of a detective's duty to inform. Together they watched the farm worker make his way over the road and onto Pencombe Farm.

"I started to look in a few places, too," volunteered Mellot.

"That's a help," said Sloan. Finding out how far a crow flew was high on his own list of priorities. There was a flourishing school of entomologists specialising in the study of insects and the dead. What he wanted was an ornithologist with a similar cast of mind. He turned aside. "Have you got a note of all of this, Crosby?"

"Yes, sir," said the constable stolidly.

"It still leaves a lot of acres," said George Mellot.

"Yours and everyone else's," said Sloan, making a comprehensive gesture that included the entire landscape. Len Hodge was walking along the footpath to the farm now. Sloan turned abruptly back to the farmer. "I'll see your neighbours now and we'll mount a search of as much ground as we can cover tomorrow morning."

The farmer nodded.

"We'll need volunteers," continued Sloan. He looked towards Gordon Briggs. "Would your society help?"

Paul Hucham received Detective Inspector Sloan and Detective Constable Crosby hospitably enough at Uppercombe Farm.

"Sorry about the muddle," he said, waving an arm to take in an uncleared table, "but I live alone and the woman doesn't come on Saturdays."

"That's all right," said Sloan easily. "We just want your permission to search Uppercombe Farm tomorrow. We're looking for human remains."

"Good grief!" exclaimed Hucham.

He was, judged Sloan, well under forty and quite good-looking in a saturnine way.

"Now if you had said a sheep," responded Hucham when the detective had explained, "I'd have been with you right away. The crows have a dead sheep down to bare bones in no time at all."

"It happens then—"

"It happens all right," replied Hucham vigorously. "My shepherd has to keep his eyes open, I can tell you. That's the worst of hill country; there's no knowing what sort of silly places a sheep will get itself into."

Sloan would have given a lot to have known what sort of place a dead man had got himself into.

Or been put.

"And if one of the flock goes missing . . ." The other man's voice trailed away.

One of the human flock had certainly done that, decided Sloan. And there was a parable, wasn't there, about the importance of the missing sheep as well as the one about the Prodigal Son.

Paul Hucham's mind was still on crows. "You can take it from me, Inspector, that we don't have any trouble with the carcass when a sheep dies."

"No?"

The sheep-farmer said grimly, "The birds see to that."

Sloan nodded. There had been a horror film once, hadn't there, about birds. None of your "pretty as a kingfisher" stuff about that, either. . . .

"I haven't noticed anything suspicious myself," said Hucham, "but there are quite a few nooks and crannies at Uppercombe and I don't get round them all, even in summer-time."

"Quite so," said Sloan neutrally.

"But search Uppercombe by all means," said Paul Hucham. "I'll give you a hand tomorrow."

Mrs. Andrina Ritchie at Stanestede Farm was just as willing. She received Sloan and Crosby in a farmhouse that had been modernised to within an inch of its life.

"Look where you like, gentlemen," she said at once. She was small and dark and attractive. "I'll tell my man that you're coming, otherwise he'll think there's something wrong."

"There is something wrong, madam," said Sloan flatly. "There's a dead body about this valley somewhere and we don't know where it is."

"Yes, of course, Inspector. I'm sorry. That was silly of me. It was just if Jenkins suddenly saw people everywhere. . . ."

"You haven't got any footpaths over Stanestede then," divined Sloan.

"Not public ones, thank goodness. Only our own farm paths."

"That explains that," said Sloan. "Now if you had a public right of way over the farm you would probably be used to people everywhere. You haven't seen any strangers, I suppose?"

She wrinkled her forehead. "I can't say that I have. Not lately. Mind you, Inspector, we're pretty isolated out here. It's not like being down in Great Rooden."

"All the more reason for noticing strangers, madam."

"Of course," she conceded at once, "but I certainly haven't. I'll ask Jenkins—"

"Jenkins is—"

"Our—my farm worker."

"I see, madam. You have just the one man here, do you?"

"I'm looking out for another," she said.

"I thought," said Sloan, digging into the recesses of his memory, "that Michaelmas was the time for that. . . ."

"Not any longer," she assured him. "Besides, as it happens I need somebody extra now."

"You do?"

She faced him squarely. "I expect George Mellot told you, Inspector."

"Told me what?"

"My husband has left me."

Sloan made a neutral noise. "No, he didn't say."

"Walked out, gone," she said, clenching and unclenching her fists. "Vanished."

"When?" enquired Sloan. He was, perforce, interested in anyone who was missing.

"June the first, it was."

The Glorious First.

"I'm not likely to forget the date," she added bitterly.

"No, madam." He cleared his throat. "Do you know why he went?"

"Her name," she said with venom, "is Beverley."

"Ah." This time Sloan made an all-purpose noise in his throat.

"That's all I know, Inspector."

"Not where she lives?"

"Calleford." She snorted. "Where the market is."

"What's that got to do with—"

"I thought he was at the market, didn't I?" she said.

"And he wasn't?"

"He was with Beverley, whoever she is," said Mrs. Ritchie savagely. She sniffed. "Now, Meg Mellot . . ."

"Yes?" Sloan was interested in anything to do with the Mellots.

"She always goes into Calleford on market-day with George. Does her shopping and has her hair done."

"And you didn't?"

"Not always." She drew herself up. "Not often enough, apparently."

"I see."

"Meg Mellot's a wise woman."

"Quite so, madam." Sloan stroked his chin. "Tell me, how exactly do you know that your husband went off with—er—Beverley?"

Her lip curled. "He left me a note, Inspector. In the real old-fashioned tradition of romantic fiction he left me a note."

All that Sloan knew about Romantic Fiction was that everything always ended happily.

Mrs. Ritchie was still speaking. "He put it in front of the kitchen clock, if you really want to know."

Sloan did not know if he really wanted to know about the absent Mr. Ritchie or not. "Did you keep the note?" he asked automatically.

"I threw it straight into the fire," she said. She gave him a challenging look. "Wouldn't you have done?"

"I don't know, madam, I'm sure." The prospect of Mrs. Margaret Sloan leaving him was not one he was in the habit of contemplating.

She tossed her head. "And I changed all the door locks. I'm not having him creeping back when he's tired of his Beverley." She gave Sloan a shrewish look. "Or when she's tired of him."

Sam Bailey at Lowercombe Farm could have stood in for John Bull any day. He only needed gaiters and he would have fitted the part perfectly. He shook his head solemnly when he heard Sloan's tale about the finger.

"I don't like the sound of that at all, Inspector. It isn't natural for some poor creature to be lying out there without a proper Christian burial." He snapped his fingers autocratically. "Elsie, a cup of tea for everyone."

It was always surprising, thought Sloan, what a comforting word "natural" was. Natural causes and natural justice both cropped up in police work.

So did tea, of course.

"How old is this finger?" enquired Mrs. Elsie Bailey anxiously. She was quite upset by the visit of the two policemen.

"We don't know for certain yet, madam."

"Very new?" she asked quickly.

"Not very new," said Sloan, "but not very old either."

"How new?" she persisted.

"Don't fuss, Elsie," said Sam Bailey. "It's nothing to do with us."

"A few weeks," advanced Sloan, "at a guess."

Mrs. Bailey's questioning subsided.

"A finger, did you say?" The portly old farmer nodded almost to himself. "I remember the days when there were always unknown men at the gate asking for work. Any work. None of this picking and choosing."

"Hirelings," said Mrs. Bailey, bustling about in spite of her grey hair. "You sit over here, Constable. The kettle won't take a minute."

"Any of them could have gone missing," said Bailey, his mind still on the past, "and nobody been any the wiser."

"I hope it's not going to be like that, sir," said Sloan.

Sam Bailey pointed to a stick in the corner of the room. "Mind you, I don't get about like I used to or I could have told you people whether or not there was a body at Lowercombe. Time was when I went over every yard myself. The best fertiliser there ever was the farmer's own two feet. That right, Mother?"

Mrs. Bailey nodded. "That's right, Sam," she murmured.

"You used to go over every yard yourself," adding almost to herself, "but not any more."

"Times change," said the farmer, "and not for the better, I might say."

Sloan was too wise to disagree with that sentiment.

"And as for young people today—" began the farmer. "Or that one."

"Now, Sam," said his wife, "don't you start—"

"Well, we don't get men asking for work like we used to do," said Bailey, momentarily side-tracked.

"No," agreed Sloan.

"More's the pity."

Sloan wasn't so sure about that.

"Likely then," deduced Bailey shrewdly, "that this finger isn't from someone casual."

"Naturally," replied Sloan smoothly, "we should be very interested in hearing about anyone who was missing."

"No one that I know about," said the older man. "The milkman's your best bet for that these days."

"True," said Sloan. Milk not taken in was the loudest signal of the twentieth century. There would, though, have been a lot of milk bottles outside the house of a person whose body had been reduced to a skeleton.

"I don't get about like I did," the farmer reminded him, "but I think we'd have heard if it had been anyone local, wouldn't we, Mother?"

"We hear most things," said Mrs. Bailey comfortably. "Good and bad."

"We should like to search Lowercombe tomorrow, all the same," said Sloan formally.

The farmer nodded. "We're not all that far from Pencombe—"

"As the crow flies," said Detective Constable Crosby.

"Come along in, Sloan," said Dr. Dabbe warmly, "and—let me see now—it's Detective Constable Crosby, isn't it?"

The two policemen advanced into the office of the consultant pathologist to the Berebury District General Hospital. Crosby was bearing a small cardboard box. He was carrying it before him like an undertaker with the ashes.

"I hear," began the doctor, "that you've got something really interesting for me."

"That depends," temporised Sloan.

"Come, come," said the pathologist with unabated geniality, "you wouldn't be disturbing my Saturday afternoon for nothing, would you?"

"No, Doctor," agreed Sloan.

Crosby laid the cardboard box on the pathologist's desk. Dr. Dabbe gently raised the lid.

"It's not a lot to go on, Doctor, a finger," began Sloan cautiously. "We realise that."

"Oh, I don't know," said Dr. Dabbe easily. "Think about Pandora."

"Just a finger," repeated Sloan. Opening Pandora's box had led to a lot of trouble, hadn't it?

"Better men than I have made do with less, Sloan."

"Have they, Doctor?"

There was a piece of a pelvic girdle once from a well in Egypt." The pathologist stroked his chin. "That was all there was to go on but it turned out to be a classic case of its kind."

"It looks a perfectly ordinary finger to me," said Sloan doggedly. He didn't like classic cases. They were for the historians and the textbooks.

"Phalanges digitorum manus," said Dr. Dabbe.

"Really, Doctor?" Sloan refused to think of it as anything except a finger.

Dr. Dabbe picked up a probe and pointed in turn to each bone. "We've got *phalanx prima, phalanx secunda* and *phalanx tertia.*"

Detective Constable Crosby got out his notebook. "Sounds like the Three Bears to me." He sniffed. "All we need is Goldilocks."

The pathologist peered at the contents of the cardboard box for a long moment and then said, "I can tell you one thing, Sloan, and that is that these metacarpals are male."

"That's a great help, Doctor," said Sloan sincerely.

And so it was. Women's lib notwithstanding, if there was crime involved then usually a dead man meant a different crime from a dead woman. It was not so much the separation of the sheep from the goats and the disappearance of the sacrificial lamb. . . .

"There is still a little hair present on the proximal phalanx," amplified Dr. Dabbe, "with male distribution."

"Ah."

"Dark hair," said Dr. Dabbe. "That means that unless it was dyed or he was totally bald, the owner of this finger will have had dark hair on his head too."

"That might help, Doctor."

The pathologist bent a little farther over the box. "Dead," he said presently, "something under a month."

Sloan motioned to Crosby to take a note.

"Give or take a week or two," said Dr. Dabbe.

Sloan nodded.

"And depending on the conditions in which it has been lying," continued the pathologist.

"Quite so," said Sloan. He was used to medical qualifications.

"I can't tell you if it has come from the south-west corner of the vineyard, Sloan," went on Dr. Dabbe, "but I can tell you that it has been in the open air."

"Not buried," said Sloan.

"And not somewhere dry enough to mummify it," said the doctor, touching the flesh with the edge of his probe. He had all the delicacy of the artist. "In fact," he said, "I should say that the damp had got at it quite a bit, too."

In its way, thought the detective inspector to himself, it was quite a virtuoso performance. . . .

"That any help, Sloan?"

"Anything," said Sloan fervently, "might help at this stage. Anything at all."

Thus encouraged the pathologist reached for a magnifying glass. He peered at the end of the fingernail. "If this is anything to go by, Sloan, you've got someone here who took normal care of his appearance."

"The trouble," said Sloan flatly, "is that we haven't got anyone here."

"Just the finger," put in Constable Crosby helpfully.

"The rest of him will be around," said the pathologist.

"Unless someone has discovered the perfect way of disposing of a body," said Sloan pessimistically.

"No," said Dr. Dabbe.

"No?" Sloan raised his eyebrows.

"The rest of him will be around," said Dr. Dabbe, switching his attention to the other end of the finger, "because this member has been disarticulated naturally."

"Naturally?" echoed Sloan. It didn't seem the right word somehow.

"Not by an instrument," said the doctor.

"Ah."

"By time and weather perhaps," qualified Dr. Dabbe, "but it hasn't been hacked off."

"We think it was picked off by a crow," said Sloan. Perhaps he should have said that earlier but the pathologist had got there on his own. "The girl who spotted it said that she was aware of them flying about overhead on the farm."

"Always plenty of crows on farms," pronounced the pathologist largely. "Nature's dustbinmen, you could call them."

"Nature's detective, in this case," remarked Crosby.

The pathologist pointed to the finger. "I shall be very surprised if the rest of this chap here isn't around somewhere."

Sloan took another, longer look in the box. In a matter of moments the pathologist had translated three small bones and a little skin from "Remains thought to be human" into "This chap here."

"Thank you, Doctor," he said sincerely.

Dr. Dabbe wasn't listening. With infinite gentleness and care he lifted the bones from their cotton-wool bed and laid them on his desk. He peered attentively at one of the joints. "He—whoever he was—had the very early beginnings of osteoarthritis, Sloan. Mind you, we nearly all have...."

Sloan had momentarily forgotten that the pathologist dealt in disease as well as death.

"Feel these chalky deposits, Sloan? That's what you would call rheumatism."

Sloan's gaze followed the pathologist's own finger. "Well, I never..."

"I'll be doing a routine test for foreign bodies and fingernail scrapings, of course," went on Dr. Dabbe briskly. "Macroscopically there aren't any but you never can tell."

"No." What the medical eye did not see the medical microscope did.

"Find the rest of him, Sloan," said the pathologist cheerfully, "and I might be able to tell you what he died from."

Detective Inspector Sloan took his reply straight from the pages of an early cookery book at the point where the author was advising on the making of hare pie. "First, catch your hare...."

FOUR

•

Steadfast in the faith

Police Constable Edward Mason might be slow. He was also sure. As soon as Detective Inspector Sloan and Constable Crosby had departed back to Berebury with the cardboard box containing the finger Mason told his wife that he was going out.

"On duty," he added as an afterthought.

Mrs. Mason nodded calmly. A pearl among women, she did not ask awkward questions about when he would be back or even mention supper-time.

"I'm just popping down to the Lamb and Flag," he said, reaching for his bicycle clips.

Even then she did not comment as many a wife would have done.

"To see a man about a man," added Mason ambiguously.

The Lamb and Flag was the only public house in Great Rooden and as such was in many respects the centre of village life—the church being open only on Sundays, so to speak. As a place where information was exchanged it came second only to the village general store and post office—but then that was presided over by a woman.

The Lamb and Flag was a long, low-jettied timber-and-brick building put up in the days of Good Queen Bess and good for a few hundred years more. Constable Mason dismounted from his bicycle and propped it against the gable wall. The inn sign swung from the overhanging gable above his head. Gaily painted, the red cross of the flag carried by the lamb went back beyond Queen Elizabeth to St. George and a medieval England of pilgrim routes for the faithful.

Mason did not spare the inn sign so much as a glance as he made his way inside. The interior of the pub was dark compared to the bright sunshine outside and he had to pause when he first entered to get his bearings. Usually Saturday evening was the busiest of the week but Constable Mason, who had arrived just after opening-time, found the landlord on his own.

"Evening, Vic," said Mason.

"Evening, Mr. Mason," said the landlord, Vic Higgins.

"Nice evening," observed the policeman, looking round. A dragon beam bisected the corner of the bar ceiling and added to the darkness of the room.

"A good time of the year is June," concurred Higgins, cautiously. He was a newcomer to Great Rooden and was still feeling his way.

Mason looked round the empty bar. "Quiet tonight, isn't it?"

"It's an away match."

"Ah, cricket..."

"They're playing over at Almstone today," said Vic Higgins. "That's why it's so quiet here."

"Can't have everything, I suppose."

"And what are you going to have?" asked the landlord pertinently.

"Nothing," said Mason, looking pious.

"That means you're on duty."

"It does," agreed Mason.

"If it's about after-hours drinking," began the landlord, "I can explain—"

"It's not," said Mason.

"What is it, then?" enquired the landlord warily.

"You had a bit of fighting in here, didn't you?"

"Oh, you heard about that, did you?"

"I hear most things," said Constable Mason placidly.

The landlord said, "It wasn't actually in here."

"Outside, then."

"Outside," conceded Victor Higgins unwillingly.

"What was it all about?"

"Can't say that I ever knew rightly." He started to polish a glass. "You know what pub fights are like."

"Tell me about this one," invited Mason.

"Not a lot to tell," said Vic Higgins. "I heard it start, of course—"

"Where?"

"In the spit and sawdust."

"The public bar," said the policeman. He was standing in the private one. On the wall someone had put up another sign altogether. It said "Whine Bar."

"I sent them outside straightaway," said the publican. "I wasn't having no fighting in my bar."

"Them?"

"There were just two of them."

"Not exactly an affray, then."

"Nothing like that," Higgins assured him. "Or I would have sent for you, Mr. Mason. You know I would," he added virtuously.

"Course you would, Vic," agreed Mason. He paused and then said, "There were just the two of them, I think you said."

"I did," said the landlord uneasily. "I didn't think anything more about it." He looked across the bar counter at the police constable. "Should I have done?"

"No reason why you should have," said Mason judicially. "At the time . . . ," he added.

"Something happened then?"

"It might have done," said the policeman. "On the other hand it might not."

"Ah," said the publican wisely.

"What were they fighting about?" pursued Mason.

"I never did get to the bottom of the trouble," said the landlord. "None of my business, of course," he added self-righteously.

"Of course," nodded Mason.

"Anyway," said Higgins, warming to his theme, "I got them both out of my bar and as far as I know they finished it off outside."

"Did they come back?"

"They did not," said the landlord firmly.

"Neither of them?"

"Not one ever and not the other that night."

"And that means . . ."

"I didn't," expanded Victor Higgins, "see the one of them again at all and the other didn't show up here for about a week afterwards. And then he kept pretty quiet about it. Sort of crept back, if you know what I mean." He gave a reminiscent chuckle. "He still had a bruise."

"'Bout when would all this have been, Vic?" asked Mason casually.

The landlord frowned. "Round about the beginning of the month, I should say."

"And the day of the week? Can you remember?"

"A Saturday," responded the other man promptly. "It was a Saturday, all right, and a home match." He wrinkled his brow still further. "I think it was the day they played Little Rooden."

"A needle match," agreed Mason, adding profoundly, "The nearer the opponent, the greater the rivalry." A grin spread over his face. "That must be somebody's law, mustn't it?"

"It's probably," opined the landlord, "why we went to war with France as often as we did."

"A Saturday, anyway, I think you said," commented Mason.

"I know it was a Saturday," said Higgins, "because this character always comes in Saturdays."

"That's the one who's been back?"

"That's right."

"Do you know him?"

"Sort of," said the landlord. "Trouble is I'm so new here that—"

"Tell me about him," invited Mason.

"Big chap," said Higgins readily. "Works up the road."

"At Pencombe?"

"I couldn't say about that but I know it's near because he's a fireman too." Great Rooden boasted a retained fire brigade whose members responded to a siren call-out. "He comes in with the rest of the crew on Tuesdays after practice as well."

Mason was too skilled to put a name in someone's mouth but he wanted to hear it spoken all the same. "Big chap," he recapitulated slowly, "probably works at Pencombe, is a retained fireman. That should be enough to—"

"Len!" exclaimed Higgins suddenly. "Len Hodge. That's his name. But who the other fellow was I couldn't begin to say. I've never set eyes on him afore or since."

"What was he like?" asked Mason curiously. "Can you remember?"

"A real wildwose," said Higgins. "Properly on the tatty side. Hadn't shaved and all that."

"Thanks, Vic, anyway. All that might be a help. You never can tell in this game."

"They had a real roughhouse in the yard, I can tell you," volunteered Higgins, more relaxed now.

"Oh?"

"We could hear them," said the landlord simply. "Hammer and tongs it was for a while and then it stopped."

"I see."

"We sort of waited for them to come back in."

"Like they do in Westerns," said the policeman.

"For a drink," said Higgins, "and a tidy-up."

"But it didn't happen?" said Mason.

"No. They must have gone off."

"Len Hodge has got a car, hasn't he?"

"If you can call it a car," said Higgins. "It's a broken-down old thing."

"Didn't you even hear a car door slam, then?" asked Mason.

"Can't say that I rightly remember," said Higgins frankly. "Not after all this time."

"Can you remember who else was here that evening?"

"Can't say I can," replied the landlord, wrinkling his brow. "Just the usual Saturday night regulars, I suppose. We don't get all that many strangers at the Lamb and Flag." He looked up. "Talking of strangers, Mr. Mason, what's happening at Pencombe tomorrow? I've had a character in here asking if his club can eat their sandwiches in my bar."

"That'll be Mr. Gordon Briggs, that will."

Higgins snorted gently. "It's a fine thing for a house that advertises good food."

"The Berebury Country Footpaths Society," amplified Mason.

"So that's who they are, is it?"

"What did you tell him?"

"That as long as they drank my beer they could do what they liked with their precious sandwiches."

"Good for you, Vic," said Mason absently.

"Seems they've got something on tomorrow at Pencombe."

"They have," said Mason briefly.

The landlord reverted to his original point. "Like I said," he repeated, "we don't get many strangers at the Lamb and Flag." He paused and said thoughtfully, "That was what was so funny about Len Hodge having a quarrel with this one."

"You must," persisted the policeman, "remember some of the people who were here the night of the fight."

"Same folk as'll be along presently," retorted the publican. "Hang about and they'll be in again. Tonight's Saturday, too, isn't it?"

"The finger," Detective Inspector Sloan reported back to Superintendent Leeyes, "is from a fully grown male."

Leeyes grunted.

"With dark hair," added Sloan.

"And?"

"And nothing, sir." Sloan tightened his lips. "That's all we've got to go on at the moment."

Superintendent Leeyes chose to be bracing. "You might have less, Sloan."

Sloan hurried on without comment. "I've had a list of missing persons pulled."

"Persons reported as missing," pointed out Leeyes with academic accuracy.

"Persons reported as missing," agreed Sloan. It was at times like these that the Police National Computer came into its own.

"With the sort of timing Dr. Dabbe is talking about," said Sloan carefully, "there are four males unaccounted for in Calleshire and a tidy number of girls." Time was a dimension in every police case.

"Girls will be girls," said Leeyes profoundly.

"And that's only in Calleshire," continued Sloan. The territorial inperative was one of the superintendent's stronger instincts. Sometimes he forgot that there was a wider world beyond the county boundary. Or even the limits of F Division.

"These four . . ." The superintendent waved a hand. "Go on."

"One old man from the mental hospital who wandered off." If Sloan had to put his money on someone this would be his choice.

"They don't lock the doors any more," said Leeyes.

"That makes it difficult to keep them in," agreed Sloan. It wasn't only in prison that locks helped those who owed a duty of care.

"And?"

"Two loving husbands and fathers who didn't come home after work."

"Swans mate for life," observed the superintendent cynically. "Very few other species do."

"Their wives usually want them back," said Sloan. Marriage was an honourable estate.

"They do," agreed Leeyes, adding sagely, "especially after they've been gone a little while."

"Yes, sir, I'm sure." Sloan couldn't decide if this was a male chauvinistic view or not. He did know though all about the value of a "cooling-off" period. All policemen did. It wasn't for nothing that prison was called the cooler.

"That's three," said Leeyes.

"One young person who left home and hasn't written."

"Only one?" said Leeyes.

"Last seen hitching his way to a pop festival."

"If that's not a fate worse than death," said Leeyes with emphasis, "I don't know what is."

"We're going to check on the loving husbands and fathers," said Sloan. "One was from Calleford and one from Luston."

Calleford was the county town where the headquarters of the police force was and Luston was Calleshire's industrial town in the north—where the trouble usually was.

"Every avenue should be explored," said the superintendent, who didn't have to explore avenues himself.

Detective Inspector Sloan recollected another avenue—a closed one, this time. "Crosby tried to get a print."

"From the finger?"

"Yes, sir." Sloan was irresistibly reminded of the picture of the Cheshire Cat in his childhood copy of *Alice in Wonderland*. All that had been there had been the head. And the grin, of course. With them now all there was was the finger. No, not the finger.

A finger.

"Well?" said Leeyes.

"No joy there, I'm afraid, sir. The skin's too far gone to take prints from."

Leeyes grimaced. "Just our luck."

"Yes, sir." It would be no good fingerprinting the houses of those missing persons that they knew about. Still less running through the records. Even if the owner of the finger had a record...

"This search, Sloan, that you've laid on..."

"All lined up for tomorrow morning, sir," responded Sloan. "All available men and the members of the Berebury Country Footpaths Society."

"Nice mixture, Sloan." He coughed. "I'm sorry I shan't be with you."

Sloan did not say anything at all. The superintendent's Sunday mornings were well known to be sacrosanct. They were spent on Berebury Golf Course.

"I'll keep in touch, of course," said Leeyes loftily.

"Of course, sir," said Sloan, his voice utterly devoid of expression.

"And you'll let me know if—er—anything turns up, won't you?"

"Immediately, sir," promised Sloan. He didn't know whether he sounded unctuous or not. He certainly meant to.

"What about leads, Sloan? Have you got any yet?"

"Just the one, sir."

"Ah . . ."

"I don't know how promising it is."

"Well?"

"There's a neighbouring farmer whose wife says he has gone off with his lady-love. . . ."

"Ha!"

"She doesn't seem to want him back."

"Don't blame her," said Leeyes robustly.

"She hadn't reported him missing."

Leeyes grunted.

"That will need checking on," said Sloan.

"Routine," declared Leeyes. "Nothing to touch it, Sloan." It was his credo.

"And so will the Mellots," said Sloan. "We'll have to find out what we can about them. Always supposing," he added, "that the owner of the finger is around on their farm. Find him, sir, and we'll be a big step further forward."

"Or backward," said Leeyes ominously. "Or backward."

After the police and the two walkers had been duly seen off Pencombe Farm George Mellot gravitated to the big kitchen. His wife was busy at the stove. She looked up as he came into the room.

"Supper'll be a little late," she said, "what with the police and everything."

"It's not the supper I'm worried about," said George Mellot. He looked suddenly much older.

"No," said Meg Mellot, brushing her hair back from her forehead. "No, I don't suppose it is."

"Tom," he said urgently. "I must talk to Tom."

"That's always easier said than done with Tom."

"You don't have to tell me that," he said. "He's my brother."

"Well, you know what he's like," she said. "He could be anywhere."

Mellot nodded in agreement. "Anywhere."

"Especially at the weekend," said Meg Mellot, putting a saucepan down.

"I'll try his house first anyway," said the farmer.

He went off in the direction of the farm office and the telephone. Hanging on the wall of the office was a large scale map of Pencombe Farm. He paused for a long moment in front of it and then he turned abruptly and picked up the telephone. He dialled a number. And then another. Presently he went back to the kitchen.

"No reply from his house," he said to his wife. "And his office doesn't know where he is."

"He's taking a real break then," she concluded. "And I'm not surprised either. Are you?"

He did not answer her directly. "I tried to speak to his personal assistant but he wasn't there either." He grimaced. "Personal assistant indeed!"

"Tom's a busy man these days," said Meg moderately.

"So am I," retorted George Mellot, "but I don't have a personal assistant."

"Oh, yes, you do," responded his wife with spirit, "but she doesn't get paid."

He smiled abstractedly, his mind elsewhere.

"Now I think about it, didn't Tom say he was going off somewhere to celebrate?" she said.

"He did," said her husband. "His exact words were, 'The strife is o'er, the battle's done.' He was in the church choir until his voice broke," he added inconsequentially. "He looked like an angel in a surplice."

"Deceptive things, surplices," observed Meg drily. "All the same I daresay Tom felt he could do with a holiday."

"After everything," said George Mellot meaningfully.

"It isn't every day," said Meg Mellot, "that you beat off a takeover bid."

"Dawn raid," said the farmer flatly. "That was what that was called."

"Dawn raid, then," she said. "It comes to the same thing in the end."

George Mellot nodded.

She pushed a saucepan over the stove. "And at the end of the day Mellot's Furnishings still belongs to the Mellots."

"And not to Ivor Harbeton."

"That's the great thing," said Meg anxiously, "isn't it?"

Her husband tightened his lips into a grimace. "It wasn't for want of trying, was it?"

She shuddered. "It was a nightmare."

"Horsewhipping," growled Mellot, "would have been too good for Ivor Harbeton."

"Business is business," said Meg Mellot. "I've heard Tom himself say that often enough."

"There are no holds barred in love, war and business," said George Mellot grimly.

She looked at him curiously. "Tom certainly found that out the hard way, didn't he?"

"You would have thought," said the farmer, "that when a man had built up a successful business that it would be safe enough."

"No," said Meg Mellot wisely, "that's precisely when it's at risk. Nobody wants to buy into a failure."

He squared his shoulders. "Ivor Harbeton wanted to buy Mellot's Furnishings. No doubt about that."

"He very nearly succeeded, didn't he?" said Meg Mellot softly.

"If he hadn't taken the heat off when he did—"

"Mellot's Furnishings wouldn't still have been Mellot's Furnishings," said his wife flatly.

"And Tom would have been out on his ear."

"That wouldn't have done for Tom," said Meg.

"No, it certainly wouldn't. He's a man of action is Tom."

She caught something in his tone and looked up. "What do you mean?"

"Exactly what I say." He added slowly, "Tom isn't a man to take anything lying down."

"George, what are you getting at?"

He voiced his thoughts unwillingly. "I just wonder why Ivor Harbeton disappeared when he did, that's all."

His wife stared at him.

FIVE

•

House of defence

"This way, everybody," shouted Gordon Briggs, waving an arm encouragingly. "Follow me."

The Sunday morning had found the members of the Berebury Country Footpaths Society assembled at the point where Footpath Seventy-nine came out of Dresham Wood and entered Pencombe Farm.

When the schoolmaster had got their attention he carried on. "Now that I've explained to you what it's all about we can get started."

The members of the Society were clustered round the stile on the Sleden-to-Great Rooden road. Gordon Briggs led the way over it.

"We're meeting the police at the farm for a briefing," he announced.

Wendy Lamport shivered. "I only hope I don't find anything."

"So do I," said her friend Helen.

"Once was enough," said Wendy.

"Although," added the other girl more thoughtfully, "if it was me lying out there I'd want someone to find me, wouldn't you?"

"I hadn't thought of that," said Wendy. All the same she still experienced a frisson of unwelcome remembrance as she set foot on Pencombe Farm again.

The other members of the society queued up to take their turn in clambering over the stile off the road and onto the footpath.

Detective Inspector Sloan stood by the barn door with Crosby and watched them approach. The walkers were a disparate group. The long and the short and the tall straggled over the footpath towards the barn. The collection of men who were waiting for them there was composed of policemen who were uniformly tall. George Mellot was present, too, and his bailiff, Leonard Hodge.

Sloan waited until they had all reached the farmyard before he addressed them. He had clambered up onto the step of a fork-life tractor to give him height.

"You are looking," he announced, "for a body that will have nearly been reduced to a skeleton." His mind drifted back to an old jingle of his own childhood that had run "The muvver was poor and the biby was thin, only a skelington covered in skin."

"It may be," he continued aloud, "partly covered—"

"The Babes in the Wood," murmured someone.

"Or," carried on Sloan valiantly, "it may just be lying in the open."

Wendy Lamport looked troubled.

"It won't be in wooded ground," said Sloan. There was something in Dresham Wood though, decided Sloan, or Len Hodge would not have gone there first yesterday afternoon. He made a mental note to check there as soon as he could.

"Whatever you do," warned the detective inspector firmly, "if you do find it, don't touch it." If he remembered rightly the unfortunate baby in the rhyme had fallen down the plug-hole.

"Dogs," said one of the walkers in an undertone to Gordon Briggs. "Why haven't they got tracker dogs?"

Briggs didn't answer.

"If you do find it just stay by it and shout," adjured Sloan. "Don't even walk about round it. That will disturb the ground."

"Clues," said another walker knowledgeably to his immediate neighbour. "That will be what they'll be looking for."

Sloan indicated the waiting members of the police force. "Wherever you are searching, there should be a policeman within earshot."

"That makes a change, I must say," said another member of the Berebury Country Footpaths Society in an aggrieved voice. He had once been mugged.

"If," continued Sloan, "you see anything in the least suspicious you should point it out to one of them."

"Kaarh, kaarh," croaked a crow above his head in antiphon. "Kaarh."

"Is that clear?" asked Sloan.

There were murmurs of assent from the walkers.

"Now we've got to be systematic," Sloan said. "A haphazard search isn't going to get us anywhere."

Gordon Briggs nodded approval. He was a methodical man himself.

"We shall take two fields at a time," announced Sloan, "and walk across them in a straight line."

"It's how they find people after an avalanche, too," said a young man in the society chattily, "except that then you have to poke through the snow." He spent his holidays at winter sports resorts.

"Remember that you should keep in line," said Sloan.

"Trust the police to say that," remarked a natural rebel in the crowd. "Step out of it and they're down on you like a ton of bricks."

"And keep your eyes open for clusters of crows," added Detective Inspector Sloan. "There's no reason why they shouldn't still be congregating round the skeleton."

Wendy Lamport shuddered. "How horrible!"

"It would mean that we'd found whoever it was, though, wouldn't it?" said her friend Helen practically.

"You," said Wendy irrefutably, "didn't see the finger."

"I think that's all," said Sloan to the walkers. The members of the police team had been briefed before the others came.

Gordon Briggs thrust his way forward to the front of the group and raised his voice. "Remember, everybody, lunch is at the Lamb and Flag in Great Rooden at twelve-thirty sharp. If we've found—ah—what we're looking for this morning, then we'll have a shortened walk this afternoon. If not, we'll keep looking. That understood, everybody?"

There were murmurs of assent from the assembled crowd.

Detective Inspector Sloan hadn't asked for questions. The one that he had had already from Len Hodge had been difficult enough to answer.

"There's crops in some of these fields, Inspector," he had said while they had been waiting for the Berebury Country Footpaths Society to arrive. "They're not all just grass, you know. What about walking over them?"

In the event it had been George Mellot who had dealt with that one.

Whilst Sloan had been marshalling his thoughts the farmer had said, "Surely there's nowhere that you haven't run over in the last few weeks, Len? Most of the fields have had a dressing of some sort."

"That's right, Mr. Mellot," said the farm worker quickly. "I hadn't thought about that."

"We can always look it up," said Mellot, "but I don't think that there's any field in crop that hasn't had a tractor over it since the beginning of the month. And you would have spotted a body, Len, wouldn't you, even from a tractor?"

"Oh, yes," said Hodge vigorously, "I would have seen a body right enough, Mr. Mellot."

"You'll be able to see which fields, of course," said the farmer to Inspector Sloan, "that they would be."

"Yes, sir," said the policeman. "Thank you."

That was a help. There were helicopters at the beck and call of the police force but they cost money. He made a mental note, all the same, that Hodge could have known where a body was for longer than anyone else.

"Maize," said Hodge. "It's mostly maize, of course."

"And that was only sown last month," pointed out George Mellot.

Sloan made a note of that.

"I don't know why we're bothering too much about walking over crops," said Mellot with a touch of bitterness in his voice. "One of the footpaths goes right through the middle of the largest field on the farm."

"Maize and all?" asked Sloan.

"Maize and all." The farmer gave a short, mirthless laugh. "I can assure you that that won't stop a dedicated walker like Gordon Briggs, Inspector. He'll stick to his rights and lead his tribe right across the growing crop to prove it's a right of way. That's what they've come for, remember."

"Footpath Seventy-nine," Sloan said. The Red Sea might have parted for Moses and the tribe of Israel: George Mellot's maize wouldn't give way for the walkers. They would trample right over it.

"Pioneers, O pioneers," said Mellot. Something of the church choir had stuck with him, too. "That's what they think they are."

"One abreast, of course," added Len Hodge. "They're not supposed to walk more than one abreast across a field in crop, are they, Mr. Mellot?"

"Huh!" said Mellot expressively, as the approaching walkers had come into view. "That'll be the day, that will."

Now Sloan watched the Berebury Country Footpaths Society walk away in an untidy straggle towards the nearest fields. The waiting policemen went with them in a neat phalanx led by Detective Constable Crosby. Constable Mason had merged into the group but Len Hodge stood out as a big man even among policemen.

"Start on Twenty Acre field first, Crosby," said Sloan, "and then the one beyond."

"Old Tree," Mellot informed him. "That's what the other field is called."

Sloan nodded briefly, his mind on an old body.

"There used to be one there—an old tree, I mean," said Mellot, "in my grandfather's day. It's gone now." He jerked his head. "They say that no family lasts longer than three oaks."

"All the fields here have names, I suppose, sir," said Sloan. Detection in the country was certainly a different kettle of fish from detection in the town.

"They do," answered the farmer. "They're all on the tithe map, of course, but they're older than that—"

They were interrupted by the distant sound of a siren. It had a galvanic effect on only one man. Leonard Hodge turned abruptly and ran at great speed back to the farm road. He flung himself into the driving seat of an old car already turned and facing the village, and set off with a screeching of tyres for Great Rooden.

"A fire somewhere," explained George Mellot calmly. "You'll hear the engine in a minute. It doesn't take them very long to turn out."

Sloan automatically took a look at his watch. He knew all about retained firemen in country areas far from full-time fire stations.

"A barn would be burnt to the ground by the time the regular fire engine got out to us from Calleford," said Mellot.

Sloan nodded. "And the Great Rooden crew all come from the village?"

"They do," said Mellot. "They won the County Shield last year for efficiency. . . . Listen!" He cocked his head to one side. "I think I can hear them starting off."

True enough, within minutes the sound of a klaxon came over the morning air. Loud at first, the noise rapidly diminished and soon fell away into complete inaudibility.

"They've gone the other way," concluded Mellot. Sloan's attention, though, had already gone back to the matter at hand. The searchers had fanned out across Twenty Acre and Old Tree fields, and begun their advance over the ground. They had their heads bent and eyes down as if in response to some invisible bingo caller. Detective Inspector Sloan and George Mellot walked over to them and brought up the rear.

"No joy, sir," reported Crosby at the end of their first
sweep over the territory. "Where now?"

Sloan pointed. "We'll take those two over there next."

"Longacre." The farmer supplied the field names. "And
Kirby's. Don't ask me who Kirby was because I don't know,
Inspector."

The mists of antiquity weren't Sloan's concern. His mind
was totally on the present. "Then we'll take the orchards," he
said. "The grass is long enough under the trees to hide a
dozen bodies."

Presently though the orchards, too, had been thoroughly
searched without success. And the next pair of fields. And the
next.

"Nothing, sir," reported Detective Constable Crosby.

There were cows in the field after that. With feminine
curiosity they approached the searchers, nuzzling their lunch-
bags and staring wide-eyed as the policemen and walkers
made their way purposefully across their field.

It was obvious from the demeanour of the group that they
had found nothing among the cows.

"We'll do the other side of the river next," decided Sloan.

A purposive sweep of the remaining fields of Pencombe
Farm yielded no sign of a body. By half past twelve Crosby
was reporting failure.

"Not a thing, sir, anywhere."

"You've looked under the hedges?"

"And in the ditches," said Crosby stolidly.

Sloan looked at the sketch map he had made with Constable Mason's help.

"It's nearly half past twelve, sir," said Crosby.

"Where's Mr. Briggs gone?" asked Sloan.

"He's just checking on a scarecrow."

"He would," said Sloan.

"A maukin, he called it."

"All right, then. Tell everyone to knock off now and be back
here by two o'clock sharp. We'll tackle Uppercombe after
lunch and then Stanestede."

"I want," said George Mellot loudly and clearly into the
telephone, "to speak to Mr. Tom Mellot, please."

He was answered in a pronounced foreign accent. "I am
the au pair," said a girl's voice.

"I know," said George Mellot patiently. "Can I speak to my brother, please?"

"'E is not 'ere," said the girl. "'E 'as gone away."

"Where is he then?"

"'E 'as gone away," said the voice again.

"So you said."

"'E 'as gone away yesterday."

George Mellot ground his teeth. "What I want to know is where he is."

"I do not know where 'e is," enunciated the voice in careful English.

"Didn't he leave an—"

"Mr. Mellot and the señora and the leetle children all go away yesterday," volunteered the voice.

"Where did they go?" asked George Mellot.

"In the car," explained the voice helpfully. "And the dog also because I am no good for walking the dog."

George Mellot heroically refrained from direct comment. "When are they coming back?" he asked instead.

The voice brightened. "When I see them."

"But—"

"That is what the señora said," insisted the au pair. "I remember she say exactly, to expect us when you see us."

Paul Hucham at Uppercombe Farm had a sheep in his arms when the search-party got to him immediately after they had eaten. His land climbed up out of the valley and was nearly all given over to sheep rearing. This, noted Detective Inspector Sloan, meant that all the grass was cropped short. Searching the ground therefore should be easier.

"Where do you want to start, Inspector?" asked Hucham. He lowered the sheep into a foldgarth and came forward to meet them.

"From where your land meets Pencombe land," said Sloan. His posse was methodically working outwards from where the finger had been found. If their search revealed nothing on Uppercombe Farm they would do the same eastwards at Stanestede and southwards at Lowercombe.

"Right," said Paul Hucham. "If you'll all follow me then . . ."

This time Detective Inspector Sloan perched on a stile to address his troops.

"Keep going," he exhorted them. "It must be somewhere."

This, he thought, was true. The administrator of the Berebury

District General Hospital had waxed eloquent on the subject of surgical waste the evening before. He had insisted to Sloan that the hospital's disposal procedures were absolutely water-tight. It hadn't been the most appropriate simile but Sloan had got the message.

The administrator had even quoted the hoary old advice churned out to generations of new house surgeons by the senior consultant when excising tissue at operation.

He always, he said, told them to divide the tissue they had taken from the patient carefully into three.

"Three?" Sloan had echoed, sounding like a comedian's feed-man in spite of himself. Had it always been "Yes, sir, yes, sir, three bags full," then?

"A piece for the pathologist..."

One for my master.

"A piece for the coroner..."

And one for my dame.

"And a piece for the nurse to throw away."

But none for the little boy who cries in the lane.

Sloan finished saying his own piece now to the assembled company and climbed down from the stile. Lunch-time spent at the Lamb and Flag had had a mellowing effect on the walkers. They were quite talkative now and noticeably more friendly to the policemen as they once more spread out over the fields.

"I suppose," said one of them (a "keep fit" fanatic if ever there was one), "that we're doing the same amount of walking as usual."

"More," said his companion morosely, "when you add up all the backwards and forwards. Like dogs," he added.

Paul Hucham kept with Sloan. "Inspector, there's a little hollow in the hillside where the sheep always go for shelter. A man might have done the same thing."

"Right, sir, we'll take a look at it, shall we?"

"I can always tell when there's a north-east wind blowing," he said. "It'll be full of sheep."

But there was nothing in Paul Hucham's little hollow.

"It was just a thought, Inspector," he said as they surveyed the dip in the hillside. "A man might have taken shelter there too."

Sloan nodded. Watching animals made sense. They said that if a man wanted to survive in the jungle he should watch what the monkeys ate. And eat the same things.

"It was worth checking, sir," he said. In some matters Sloan was definitely on the side of the apes and not the angels.

Paul Hucham frowned. "I can't think of anywhere else at Uppercombe where a skeleton might be other than on open ground. There's no shelter to speak of at all up here."

"We'll find it, sir, never worry," said Sloan. "Just give us time, that's all. It's not going to run away," he added grimly. "That's for sure."

"No," said the farmer. He turned. "We'll have to cut back this way, Inspector, because of the stream."

"Where does this one go? Down to the Westerbrook?" There was a narrow footpath running down beside the little stream.

Hucham shook his head. "No. This flows down through Stanestede Farm. It gets bigger farther down the hill. It's very important to the Ritchies there."

"They get their water from it, do they?" In the town water came in pipes but Sloan could quite see that matters might be different out here in the country.

"Their electricity," said Hucham. "They've got a generator just above the farm. That's how they're able to be all electric there without it costing them anything."

"Nice for them," said Sloan, householder. "What about you?"

"I have to make do with the view," said Paul Hucham, waving an arm. "It's not bad, is it?"

"It's very fine," said Sloan.

"On a clear day you can see Calleford."

Sloan nodded and turned to look back down at Pencombe Farm set at the bottom of the valley. Below them a determined search of Uppercombe Farm was being carried on. Once he caught the sound of Detective Constable Crosby's voice borne upwards by the wind. Even at a distance he could pick out Gordon Briggs hurrying about as fussy as a sheep-dog. Over on his right the river Westerbrook glinted as the sun caught the moving water. He made a mental note to make sure that the banks of the river had been properly checked. Dr. Dabbe had mentioned that the finger had been somewhere where the damp could get at it, hadn't he?

"Plenty of crows up here, Inspector," remarked Hucham presently.

Sloan turned his attention to the sky. True enough, there were crows about. Their shiny black plumage was quite unmistakable. He looked at them keenly. Any one of them could have dropped the finger in front of the two walkers. And one of them, Sloan reminded himself, knew where the body of a man was to be found even if he, Sloan, didn't.

"Kaarh, kaarh, kaarh," called a crow hoarsely.

"It must be lonely for you up here, sir," remarked Sloan.

"The winter drags a bit," admitted the sheep-farmer, "until the lambing starts. After that I'm too busy to notice."

"And then suddenly it's spring, I suppose," said Sloan absently. He could see that the latest cast by the search-party below had drawn a blank. Crosby was waving his arm and slowly all his helpers started to drift down the hillside again, this time in the direction of Stanestede Farm. Sloan turned to Paul Hucham. "Thank you, sir."

"Sorry you didn't have any luck, Inspector."

"It's not for want of trying," said Sloan. He regarded the landscape laid out below him. "And somewhere down there is what we're looking for."

"I'd rather someone else found it, all the same," said the other man with a rueful half-laugh.

"Yes, sir," responded Sloan philosophically. There were some jobs that society was always content to have done for it by someone else. And the police force collected quite a lot of them.

"It's all very well when it's only a sheep," said Paul Hucham. "A human being is a different proposition altogether."

"That's why we're searching the land now," said Sloan. It must have been quite a benchmark of civilisation when early man had begun to bury his dead. Now he came to think of it, the act of burial was one of the things which separated man from beast.

"Of course," said Hucham uneasily.

"We couldn't do nothing," said Sloan as much to himself as to the farmer. "Not once we knew." Except elephants. He was forgetting that they buried their fellow elephants when they died, too, didn't they?

"Of course not," agreed the farmer hastily. "That wouldn't do at all."

They had even, Sloan remembered, his thoughts running silently on, found time to bury that chap "whose corse to the rampart we hurried." And that had been in the heat of battle. Sir John Moore after Corunna. Never mind that not a drum was heard, not a funeral note: that wasn't what had been important. What had mattered was that the old warrier hadn't been left lying around for the crows.

Filled with new resolve Sloan turned and took his leave of the sheep-farmer.

SIX

•

A perfect end

Mrs. Andrina Ritchie received the policemen and the walkers at Stanestede Farm. She was dressed for the town, not the country. And for Sunday, too.

"You won't mind if I don't come with you, will you?" she said to Detective Constable Crosby, who had led the way there.

"No, madam," said that worthy with absolute truth. Well-dressed women frightened him. His gaze drifted involuntarily down to her feet. In his opinion Mrs. Ritchie's shoes came into the category of foot ornaments rather than useful articles. They would not have stood up to life on the farm for very long.

"Go wherever you please," she said, waving an arm to encompass the land. "It's all the same to me."

"Thank you, madam." Crosby cleared his throat: he had been instructed to ask an important question. "Do you keep pigs at Stanestede, by any chance?"

"Pigs? Certainly not. Nasty, messy creatures." She looked at him. "Why do you want to know that?"

"Just checking, madam, that's all." The detective constable made a note in his book. Pigs were omnivorous. That, as Detective Inspector Sloan had carefully explained to him, meant that they ate everything.

But everything.

"We've only got cattle here," she said.

"I see," said Crosby. Cattle were more selective. They didn't eat everything.

"They're bad enough," said Mrs. Ritchie.

"I'm sure they are," responded Constable Crosby, townee. Actually the police weren't interested in cows, although he did not say so. What they were worried about was pigs. Eating people was wrong but pigs did not seem to know this. Cattle did.

"Cows are always needing looking after," she said resentfully, patting her hair with one hand. "I'm going to give them up

53

now that I'm on my own and go over to sheep. They're a lot less trouble."

"I'm sure that there'll be changes at Stanestede," murmured Crosby diplomatically.

"You can bet your life there will," she said, tightening her lips. "I like a weekend to be a weekend."

So did Crosby.

"And with stock," said Andrina Ritchie, "it isn't."

"No, madam." It wasn't with crime either but he did not say so.

"Now, Officer, what do you want from me?"

"Did your husband—" Crosby stopped and started again. "Have you got a large scale map of the farm anywhere?"

"In the office," she said. "On the wall. This way."

She led Crosby through the house and into the kitchen. The farm office at Stanestede was in a little room off the kitchen, accessible from the out-of-doors as well. The constable stared at the kitchen. It couldn't have been in greater contrast to the one at Pencombe Farm. Here there was no welcoming fire, no vast scrubbed elm table—just a formidable collection of electric machines arrayed in clinical grandeur amid a lot of colourful formica. The whole ensemble might have come from the pages of a women's magazine. There was no touch of the country farmhouse kitchen about it at all.

"Nice, isn't it?" said Mrs. Ritchie, pausing for a moment on the way through. The kitchen was obviously something she prized. "We have our own electricity at Stanestede, you see. There's a stream," she added vaguely.

Crosby could pick out the stream on the map of the farm. On the fields on the map was pencilled in the current crop, and the date of sowing, and where the cows were now pastured and where they had been.

"We're not allowed to grow too many potatoes," said Mrs. Ritchie. "I do know that."

Crosby wondered what else this fashionably dressed creature knew about running a farm.

"Just our share," she said.

Against one field on the map Crosby saw written a word that he had not expected to see.

"Beg pardon, madam," he said, pointing.

"What?"

"There."

"Rape," she said.

"That's what I thought it was," said Crosby.

"Oil-seed rape," she said.

"Ah," he said delicately. "And what—er—sort of rape is oil-seed?" Back at the police station they just had the one variety of rape on the books. Not that that saved any trouble. Hard to prove and even harder to defend: that was the problem with a charge of rape. Experienced police officers suddenly found themselves urgently needed elsewhere when one was in the offing.

"For the cows to eat," added Mrs. Ritchie.

His face cleared.

She gave him an appraising glance. "Thought fields of rape were just another of our little country ways, did you?" she said. "Like a maypole."

"It's a difficult subject," said Crosby, discomfitted. That was one thing that was dinned into all police constables at their training school. It wasn't so much the "heads I win, tails you lose" odds that went with getting involved with the charge of rape as the "Stop it, I like it" dialogue invariably reported by the defence and advanced in amelioration. Even when the victim was as badly mauled as a mating mink. The dialogue reported by the prosecution was usually as totally disconnected as the "And he said" and then the "And she said" sequence when the paper was turned over in a game of Consequences.

"I wouldn't know anything about rape," said Mrs. Ritchie drily. "All I can tell you, Officer, is that now I know what that person meant who said something about hell having no fury like a woman scorned."

"That's the other side of the coin, madam, isn't it?" said Crosby gravely. "How are you managing on your own?"

"Everyone is being very kind," she replied. "I don't know where I would have been without my neighbours. Paul and George have both been very good to me."

"That'll be Mr. Hucham and Mr. Mellot, won't it?"

"I don't know where I would have been without them," she said, nodding, "and even old Mr. Bailey said if I needed any advice I wasn't to hesitate to ask him."

"A bit set in his ways, isn't he?" ventured Crosby. That much had been evident on one visit to Lowercombe Farm.

"You can say that again," said Mrs. Ritchie wryly. "Things

haven't changed at Lowercombe since Nelson lost his eye. No wonder Luke couldn't stand it."

"Luke?" That was a new name to Crosby.

"His son. Luke Bailey. His father drove him too hard." Andrina Ritchie gave a brittle laugh. "And he drove him to drink in the end."

"Did he, madam?" That explained an old man working long after he should have been sitting by the fireside in his slippers.

"So they say." She shrugged her shoulders. "I haven't seen him in years. I shan't be taking his father's advice but it was nice of him to offer, wasn't it?" She favoured the constable with a tight smile "Anyway, I've got a good man working for me and that makes a difference."

Crosby agreed warmly that it did and finished his survey of the wall map.

"I think that's all I need to see for the time being, madam, thank you, before we begin our search. We'll let you know if we should find anything at Stanestede."

Mrs. Andrina Ritchie shuddered delicately.

If the state of his temper was anything to go by, Superintendent Leeyes had not won his golf match.

"Nothing?" he barked down the telephone from the clubhouse.

"Nothing, sir," reported Detective Inspector Sloan. "We've searched two of the farms within our radius now and there are two more to go."

"Dormy."

"Pardon, sir?"

"Nothing." Leeyes grunted. "A crow doesn't fly all that far, surely?"

"No, sir." How far crows flew had been one of the things that Sloan had had to find out the evening before.

"And a human skeleton is a big thing."

"Yes, sir."

"It must be somewhere," insisted Leeyes. He was not at his postprandial best. He rarely was after a luncheon taken at the nineteenth hole of the golf-course.

"Sir." Sloan went off at a tangent. "Constable Mason has reported that one of the men out here had a bust-up with a stranger—"

"Hasn't made an arrest in years, hasn't Mason," complained Superintendent Leeyes in an aggrieved tone of voice.

"It was in the local pub," persisted Sloan. "It's called the Lamb and Flag."

"Trust Mason not to—"

"It happened about a month ago," went on Sloan valiantly. "The man was all cherried up at the time, he says."

"What man?" asked Leeyes, his wayward attention engaged at last.

"Leonard Hodge," replied Sloan. "He's George Mellot's farm bailiff. Big fellow," he added. It was something worthy of note. Most criminals were smaller than most policemen. Sloan didn't know if this was because policemen had to be tall to be policemen or that criminals came up particularly small, but as a rule they did. A rule of thumb, that is. A rule of Tom Thumb, you might say.

Leeyes groaned. "You'd better look into that, Sloan, hadn't you? And, Sloan . . ."

"Sir?"

"Mellot's Furnishings. You said it rang a bell."

"I thought," said Sloan cautiously, "that I remembered having seen something about them in the papers recently."

"You had," said Leeyes.

"Because they're so well known, I suppose."

"They've been in the news all right, Sloan." He sounded grim.

"I thought I'd read—"

"This," said Leeyes meaningfully, "had spilled over from the financial pages."

"That explains it then, sir," said Sloan with some satisfaction. "What was it, do you know?"

"An attempt to take over the firm."

"So it was," said Sloan, metaphorically slapping his thigh. "I remember now. I knew I'd seen the name lately."

"An attempt to take over the firm," reiterated Leeyes, "and oust Tom Mellot as chairman."

"The brother?"

"Precisely, Sloan," said Leeyes. "It began," he informed him, "with the usual thing."

"What was that, sir?" Sloan did not pretend to be a financier.

"Buying up Mellot's shares quietly and then not so quietly."

"I see."

"And then a cash offer," said Leeyes, "at an offer price in excess of the market price of the shares."

"Sounds fair enough," said Detective Inspector Sloan, simple policeman.

"Or rather," qualified Leeyes, "a cash adjustment and loan stock in the acquiring company."

"I suppose that depends on how good a proposition the acquiring company is," responded Detective Inspector Sloan, not-so-simple policeman.

"Very probably," said Leeyes. "Anyway, in theory they only need to get the consent of fifty-one percent of the shareholders—it's usually less in practice—and Bob's your uncle."

Sloan translated this. "New management."

"It would have been the end of Tom Mellot as chairman anyway."

"Would have been, sir?" he queried.

"Didn't you hear the end of the story, Sloan?"

"Can't say that I did, sir." Something else must have become a nine-days' wonder in the newspaper instead. "Not that I noticed anyway."

"The company doing the taking over..." Leeyes paused impressively.

"Yes?"

"They were called Conway's Covers."

"Were they, sir?" Sloan had forgotten the details. "Was that important?"

"It belonged to Ivor Harbeton, the financier."

"But, sir," said Sloan involuntarily, "he's disappeared. Everyone knows that."

The disappearance of Ivor Harbeton wasn't a nine-days' wonder. That had been a big news story. The Harbeton financial empire touched commercial life at many points. Ivor Harbeton's interests spread out through industry like the threadlike filaments of honey fungus. The City had been shaken by his sudden absence from the helm, and the ominous word "Levanter" had been hinted at in some suspicious-minded quarters. A deputy chairman was in the saddle, making prevaricating noises. Of Harbeton himself there was no sign.

"Precisely, Sloan," said Leeyes. "I'm having them gather all the newspaper cuttings together for you now at the station."

"For me, sir?"

"For you, Sloan," said Leeyes heavily. "Just in case."

*   *   *

Sam Bailey waved his stick. "I'm sorry I can't come with you, Inspector, I'm not the man I was."

"That's all right, sir."

"Once upon a time I'd have got to the top of the combe before any of you young chaps."

"I'm sure you would, sir."

"My wife'll set you on your way, though." He trundled off down the hallway shouting, "Elsie, where are you? Elsie, I want you!" When there was no response to this cavalier summons he grumbled, "She's never around these days. Spends all her time messing about in the kitchen." He stumped back up the hall to the policemen, chuckling grimly. "I never missed a hunt if I could help it."

"No, sir."

"Of any sort." He waved his stick again. "This is Tuesday country."

"Tuesday country, sir?" echoed Sloan blankly.

"The South Calleshire Fox Hunt, Inspector."

"Ah." Sloan's brow cleared.

"They meet at Great Rooden on Tuesdays."

"Really, sir?" The police hunt met on Saturdays usually.

"Outside the Lamb and Flag at eleven," said the old farmer. "I must say they used to do a very good stirrup-cup in Rodgers's day. I don't know what the new man there is like."

With the police it was under the railway arches at Berebury in the evening. That was where their quarry was most often to be found. And they didn't have a stirrup-cup beforehand. All they ran to was a pint or two of beer afterwards.

"They usually find quite quickly," said Bailey.

So did the police.

"Good hunting country, Inspector, this."

"Yoicks, tally-ho," said Detective Constable Crosby to nobody in particular.

The rallying call of the police was "Calling all cars."

"From a find to a check," wheezed Bailey.

With the police from a find to a check meant the plaintive call sign "I am in need of assistance."

"From a check to a view," said Bailey neatly. "That's what you want, isn't it, Inspector? A view..."

"It would be a great help."

"I saw you on the hill." He grunted. "Nothing wrong with my eyesight."

"We drew a blank." Sloan found himself lapsing into the vernacular.

"I knew you hadn't found at Uppercombe or Stanestede," said the farmer, "or you wouldn't be here at Lowercombe."

"No, sir."

"From a view to a death." He looked at the policeman abruptly. "I take it you know your 'John Peel,' don't you, Inspector?"

"Yes, sir." All schoolboys kenned John Peel with his coat so gay. It was about all that most of them did know about hunting, too.

"'Peel's view-hallo would waken the dead,'" quoted the old farmer chestily.

"Not this dead, it wouldn't," interposed Detective Constable Crosby. "You see—"

"Suppose," said Sloan swiftly, "we start with those meadows over there and then go on to the wood—"

Sam Bailey waved his stick. "Go where you like, Inspector, but don't count on too much."

"What do you mean?"

"I told you that this is good hunting country."

"So you did, sir."

"That means," amplified Bailey, "that there are plenty of foxes about."

"Well?"

"They don't mind what they eat." He sniffed. "Reynard's not particular at all, if you take my meaning. If they've got at your man I can tell you they'll have made a real mess of him."

Sloan cast his gaze over the pastoral valley of the Westerbrook and the four comfortable farms within the self-imposed—crow-imposed—ambit of police investigation. Whoever it was had said "Though every prospect pleases, and only man is vile" was wrong. Nature was red in tooth and claw, too. Tooth as well as claw, you might say, if foxes as well as crows were having their way with the body of a man. It was an unattractive thought. At least none of the farmers kept pigs. That was something for an investigating officer to be profoundly thankful for. He braced himself. "Come along, Crosby."

Crosby squared his shoulders and went off to round up his helpers.

"Make a good whipper-in, that lad," remarked Sam Bailey appraisingly.

It wasn't the similarity to the hunt that was to the forefront

of Sloan's mind as he stood on the front doorstep of Lowercombe
Farm and watched the searchers fan out over Sam Bailey's
fields. It was the word "dragnet" that he thought about. A
trawl over land. Somewhere out here, little foxes notwithstanding, were the remains of a human being. There must be.

"Has he been blooded?" Sam Bailey interrupted his thoughts.

"What—I beg your pardon, sir?"

"Made his first arrest," said the farmer. "That young fellow
with you."

"Oh, yes, sir." Making an arrest wasn't what Sloan would
call being blooded. Initiation rites in the police force were
more rigorous than that. Breaking bad news called for more
courage. So did pacing a lonely beat at two o'clock of a
winter's morning when all was patently not well. To say
nothing of attending a raging "domestic" when the man was
roaring drunk and the woman a screaming virago, hell bent
on exacting vengeance on her man.

On any man.

On the nearest man.

He answered Sam Bailey quite seriously, "He's been blood-
ied, too, if it comes to that."

Sam Bailey nodded.

Perhaps, thought Sloan, that was where the line lay between the new policeman and the seasoned one. After the
moment when a member of that very same public whose civil
rights you had sworn upon oath to uphold hit you rather
hard where it hurt. Most policemen took a different view
after that.

"He's had his brush then, has he?" said Sam Bailey.

"With a villain or two," replied Sloan.

"Doesn't look old enough to me."

"He is," said Sloan tightly. The master gave the tail of the
fox—the brush, that is—to the youngest member of the hunt
present, didn't he? Sloan pursed his lips. It wasn't like that in
the police force. There the greenhorn got the clerical work
and the kicks.

"Mind you," said the old farmer, "I've got to the age now
when policemen get younger every year." He looked round
irritably. "Where is that wife of mine?" He turned and
shouted down the hall again.

"It happens to us all," responded Sloan more equably. He
had noticed that the walls of Lowercombe Farm were peppered
with stuffed heads of foxes; weren't they called masks? They

had a different set of trophies down at the police station. No
more arcane, of course. Some closed files, for instance; a
commendation or two from the bench of magistrates; a few
kind words from a judge; more satisfying, a menace to society
behind bars for a tidy while, and little old ladies able to walk
through the streets at night—if that was what they felt like
doing.

"You'll let me know, Inspector, won't you," said Bailey,
latter-day John Peel, "if you find anything at Lowercombe?"

"You'll hear all about it, sir, I promise you," said Sloan,
preparing to stride off to join Crosby and the rest of the
search-party.

They were interrupted by the arrival of Mrs. Bailey, who
came hurrying down the farmhouse hall all breathless and
flustered, taking off her apron as she advanced towards them.
"Good afternoon, Inspector Sloan."

"Ah, there you are, Elsie." Her husband banged his stick
crossly on the floor. "Where have you been?"

"In the larder," said Mrs. Bailey, putting her apron on a
chair and turning to Sloan. "I'm sorry, Inspector, not to have
been here when—"

"Didn't you hear me calling you?" demanded Sam Bailey.
"I shouted quite loudly."

"I'm sure you did, Sam," Elsie Bailey said drily, "but I had
the larder door closed and it was only when I got back to the
kitchen and heard you talking that I realised that someone
was here."

"I was just going," said Sloan, not dissatisfied with his visit
to Lowercombe Farm. Hounds followed a trail by scent:
policemen followed one compounded of information and
observation—and deduction. If Mrs. Bailey had been in the
farmhouse larder when her husband had first called her Sloan
was prepared to eat his proverbial hat.

Unless, that is, the larder had a carpet of leaf-mould.
Because that was undoubtedly what was sticking to Mrs.
Elsie Bailey's shoes.

SEVEN

•

Have mercy upon us

Police Constable Ted Mason might be one for the quiet life.
That was not to say that he was not also a conscientious police
officer. He was not an unclever one either. He unobtrusively
absented himself from the search-party working its way over
Lowercombe Farm and slipped back into the village. This
time he did not choose the Lamb and Flag public house as
his source of information. He made his way instead to Great
Rooden's village store and post office. If nothing else, as
Superintendent Leeyes had remarked, he knew his patch.

He began with an apology. "Sorry to be knocking you up
on a Sunday afternoon, Mabel," he said.

"That's all right, Ted," was the calm reply. As the principal
shopkeeper in Great Rooden Mrs. Mabel Milligan was an
important figure in the social fabric of the village. Being
disturbed out of shop hours was part of the price she paid for
her importance. "What can I get you?"

"Sugar," responded Police Constable Mason promptly.

Now Mrs. Mabel Milligan had personally served Mrs.
Mason with two kilos of cane sugar and ten of preserving
sugar for jam-making—strawberries being nearly ready for
this—only the day before but she did not say so. "What sort of
sugar?" she enquired instead, taking it that the Sunday
Trading Act was not going to be mentioned by either party.

"Ordinary sugar," replied Mason, momentarily flummoxed.

Mrs. Milligan led the way through into the darkened store
and picked out a bag of cane sugar for him. "Can't have you
running out, can we?" she observed drily.

"No." Ted Mason handed over the money for the sugar,
remarking with apparent inconsequence, "I've been at
Pencombe all day; otherwise I would have come earlier."

"They're having a bit of trouble over there, I hear," rejoined
Mrs. Milligan.

The constable nodded. "There's probably a dead man
about somewhere." He did not immediately expand on this.

He knew that Mrs. Milligan's intelligence-gathering network was at least as good as his own and there was no point in telling her anything that she already knew.

"From all accounts," said Mrs. Milligan circumspectly, "he's been there a tidy old time too."

"'Bout a month," volunteered Mason. There was no secret about that.

"Dear, dear," clucked Mrs. Milligan, "that's bad."

"Doesn't make detecting any easier," agreed the grower of prize cabbages.

"It can't do, Ted," responded Mrs. Milligan warmly. "A month. Fancy that."

"Lost any customers lately, Mabel?" The policeman was quite serious now.

She frowned. "Charlie Gibbs—he died, didn't he? About the beginning of June, that would have been."

"I saw him buried myself," said Ted Mason, "seeing as how he used to grow marrows."

"They had a ham," remarked Mrs. Milligan inconsequentially.

The policeman nodded. The purchase of funeral baked meats came close to circumstantial evidence of burial.

"There was old Miss Tebbs, too."

"Another ham?" enquired Mason without irony.

Mabel Milligan sniffed. "Her nephew didn't even have a tea."

"Always was a mean man, was Albert Tebbs, and he hasn't changed as he's got older."

"People don't," said Mrs. Milligan sagely. "They just get more like they were before."

"Albert Tebbs will die rich," forecast Mason.

Mrs. Milligan's mind was on something else. "You could say," she murmured delicately, "that in a manner of speaking I'd lost another customer as well."

Police Constable Mason waited.

"Mr. Ritchie." She pursed her lips. "You know about Mr. Ritchie, don't you?"

He nodded. "We had heard."

"Not that Mrs. Ritchie has made any secret about it. 'No more bacon, Mrs. Milligan,' she said to me the first time she came in after he'd gone. 'Nasty, fattening stuff.'" Mrs. Milligan looked down at her own ample figure and went on. "Myself, I must say I like a nice slice of best greenback to start the day."

"Me, too," agreed the portly policeman absently. He reverted to Martin Ritchie. "Gone off with a girl, I hear."

"So Mrs. Ritchie said." Mrs. Milligan tossed her head. "Can't say I blame him for that. Nothing to come home to there in the way of home comforts."

"She doesn't look a good cook," ventured Mason with all the authority of a man long married to a very good cook indeed.

Mabel Milligan, no mean trencherwoman herself, waved a pudgy hand. "She isn't. She was always buying made-up dishes."

Ted Mason regarded her with respect. "You know all about us, don't you, Mabel?"

"A man is what he eats," she said profoundly.

"And you," said the policeman neatly, "know what everyone in Great Rooden eats, don't you?"

She squinted modestly at the shop floor. "Can't help it, can I? You see everything from behind the counter."

"And you don't let on, do you?" he said. Mrs. Milligan had a great reputation in Great Rooden for keeping her own counsel.

"I never was one to talk, Ted Mason," she retorted briskly, "and well you know it."

"So that's three customers you've lost in June," he said, changing his tack a little.

"Some you gain, some you lose," she said cryptically. "There's swings and roundabouts in everything."

"No one else missing, anyway?" said the policeman.

"Nobody buying for one that used to buy for two, if that's what you mean," she countered precisely.

"Except Mrs. Ritchie?"

"Buy!" echoed Mrs. Milligan richly. "That woman doesn't buy. She only picks about. She's that keen on her precious figure that she doesn't buy proper food at all."

"We're looking for Martin Ritchie anyway, just to check up." Mason transferred the bag of sugar to his other hand. "Talking of checking up . . ."

"Yes?" It was the tribute of one well-informed villager to another and she knew it.

"I hear that Len Hodge had a bit of an up-and-downer in the Lamb and Flag last month."

"Did he?" Mabel Milligan's face was expressionless.

"It's not like him," observed Mason.

"No," she agreed with this. "He's not a fighter, isn't Len."

"I just wondered..." began Mason.

"Yes?"

"If you had heard who it was that he was fighting with."

"Me?" she said blandly. "Why ask me? Why don't you ask Vic Higgins? He's the landlord."

"Because he's new, that's why."

She shifted her ground. "Now, how should I know what goes on at the Lamb and Flag?"

"Because, Mabel," replied Mason cogently, "you hear everything that goes on in Great Rooden, that's why."

"So do you, Ted Mason."

"No, I don't," he said simply. "I'm a policeman, remember. I only hear what people want me to hear." He transferred the bag of sugar back to his other hand. "There's some things that get kept from me."

"Are there now?" she said tonelessly.

"If people think it's better that I don't know about something then they don't tell me."

"Well, then—"

"Which is not the same thing at all," persisted the policeman, standing the bag of sugar on the counter, "as telling me and trusting that I'll do the right thing."

She nodded. "I can see that."

"So," he said judiciously, "if you should happen—just happen, mind you—to hear who it was that Len Hodge was fighting with in the Lamb and Flag that night I'd be greatly obliged if you'd let me know."

Mrs. Milligan remained impassive. "I'll remember that, Ted."

"Because if it's anything to do with this dead man that's around somewhere we're going to find out sooner or later anyway."

"Course you are," she agreed.

"And then," insisted the policeman heavily, "it'll be a lot easier for everybody concerned if it's been sooner rather than later."

Mrs. Milligan let him get as far as the shop door before she spoke. "You've forgotten the sugar, Ted," she said. "That was what you came for, wasn't it?"

Detective Inspector Sloan let the crowd of walkers and policemen fan out over Lowercombe Farm without him. He had gone with them a little way—just until he was out of sight of the farmhouse and Mr. and Mrs. Bailey, who were standing together at the front door. Side by side the old couple looked like Darby and Joan but Sloan kept an open mind about this. Oedipus and several schools of articulate European psychologists had had a lot to say about the lasting outcome of parent-and-child relationships. They were much less eloquent in their pronouncements on the long-term effects of those between husband and wife.

Perhaps it wasn't so important after all but before now Sloan had noticed that the ways of the partner opposite the forceful one of the pair often ran very deep indeed. A lifetime spent outwardly agreeing with Sam Bailey would surely have made its mark on any woman. He knew from his own experience in the force that instant obedience was no criterion of genuine compliance—nor of anything but token subservience to an authority that it would be imprudent to challenge. Sam Bailey, crossed, would obviously be a very awkward customer indeed.

Once all the others had turned the corner from the farmhouse Sloan hung back and soon the rest of the search-party were way ahead of him. That was when he turned in his tracks and made steadily for Dresham Wood. It lay behind the farmhouse, sheltering it from the hill behind and coming between the road and the farm proper. Lowercombe, being at the bottom of the valley, was in by far the most favoured position of all the farms. The river Westerbrook flowed through this land, too. It was a little fuller down here than it was higher up the hill and Sloan could see the blue forget-me-nots growing in the banks and a flower that might have been purple loosestrife not far from the water's edge.

He soon picked up the track into the wood that was obviously Footpath Seventy-nine. There was no mistaking it—the Berebury Country Footpaths Society would have had little problem in identifying their trail where it led into the wood. The way through the trees was well defined, too, although here and there young branches had grown across the route, and the odd bramble had sent out a new spur which lay in wait for the unwary. It didn't catch Sloan because he had his eyes down anyway. Leaf-mould there was in plenty under the canopy of the trees but it lay to the sides of the path.

He did cast his eyes upwards a couple of times to see what manner of wood Dresham was. In the main it was oak and ash

trees which met his gaze, though he caught sight of a thorn or
two and a holly. As he advanced farther into the wood he
came across a wild cherry and he thought he saw the greenish
white of a guelder rose. There was a great deal of undergrowth, too. Too much. Far too much, in fact. Sam Bailey
wasn't tending his land as he should. Sloan saw several dead
trees that should have been out of the wood and burnt a
couple of years ago at least, and others that should have been
felled in their prime for timber. Woods needed culling in the
same way that herds of deer did.

At one point quite soon after he had entered the wood the
footpath crossed a tiny runnel of water finding its immemorial
way down to the Westerbrook—too slight even to call for
stepping-stones where the path crossed it. Everyone was
obviously left to pick their own way over the dampness as
best they could. They had done so by stepping to one side of
the path or the other and selecting the best place to stride
across. There the path showed footmarks in plenty. Detective
Inspector Sloan regarded them with an automatic professional
interest. Mrs. Elsie Bailey was short but not thin. Any
footprint that she made in soft ground would be small but
deep. One look at the multitude of footmarks in the damp
ground disabused him of the hope that he would find any
one print without a lot of trouble—and luck. He would have
to seek another way of finding out what it was that Mrs.
Bailey had gone into the wood for.

And Len Hodge.

Sloan penetrated farther but was no wiser. There was
enough undergrowth to conceal almost anything from sight
from the path. If there was a woodland grave hereabouts he,
Sloan, wasn't going to find it single-handed. If, though, a fox
had found it first, then a finger might well have been dropped
on open ground by Master Reynard, and then been found by
a crow. That wouldn't be so much an ecological coincidence as
the sort of chain of circumstances greatly beloved by legal
counsel for whomsoever they were acting. Chains of circum-
stance left plenty of room for manoeuvre in court.

He carried on, his mind a confusion compounded of childhood recollections of the deceptively simple tale of the Babes
in the Wood—if ever a case had called for a full-scale police
investigation it was the nasty story of the Babes in the
Wood—whatever had their parents been thinking of—and
that sinister ballad "The Twa Corbies." Although it had been

about ravens rather than crows, there was a dreadful relevance about the birds asking each other where they would go
and dine today.

At one point Sloan stopped and stood still for a minute or
two and listened. If his eyes could not supply him with any
clues perhaps his ears could. But he was aware of nothing
except the alarm call of a bird which had heard him approaching
and was uttering a general warning.

He pushed on again.

The undergrowth was right up to the path now, and he
could see almost nothing through it. It would need a great
deal of time and men to search the wood properly. In "The
Twa Corbies" the new-slain knight whose body had provided
dinner for the ravens had been lying behind the old turfed
bank. . . .

>   And naebody kens that he lies there,
>   But his hawk, his hound, and his lady fair.

Sloan would very much have liked to know if the same
could be said of the owner of the finger that now reposed in
Dr. Dabbe's forensic laboratory. He would also have liked to
know—and had every intention of finding out—what it was
that had brought Len Hodge and Mrs. Elsie Bailey into
Dresham Wood so urgently. He forged on without coming
any nearer to knowing and after a while started to see the
trees beginning to thin out ahead.

Through the wood without being out of it yet, he thought
to himself, turning and retracing his steps back to the farmyard at Lowercombe.

The others didn't find anything on Sam Bailey's land even
though they searched all over it until the end of the afternoon.

Gordon Briggs, self-appointed spokesman of the Berebury
Country Footpaths Society, reported failure to Sloan with
melancholy satisfaction. "Nothing, Inspector. Not a sign of
anything suspicious."

"Somewhere," said Sloan determinedly, "within the radius
that we have been searching is a skeleton." A crow would not
fly over a greater acreage than they had walked over that
afternoon with something relatively heavy in its beak. The
ornithologist had said so.

"Very likely," responded Gordon Briggs, "but my members
haven't found it yet and neither have your policemen." He

looked rather pointedly at his watch and coughed. "Mrs. Mellot kindly said she would give us tea."

Sloan bowed to a higher reality and when Detective Constable Crosby's team, too, gave Lowercombe Farm a clean bill of health he consented to a general return across the road and back to Pencombe Farm. There was someone else making his way back there at the same time. Just as the walkers reached the farmyard they were overtaken by Len Hodge in his disreputable old car. As the farmworker clambered out one of the walkers said to him, "You timed that nicely, didn't you, mate? Missing all the footslogging...."

Len Hodge grimaced. "Footslogging would have been easier."

"Oh?"

Hodge shrugged his shoulders. "A character over at Sleden thought the best way of getting a bonfire going when there wasn't any wind was to pour a can of paraffin over it."

"Oh, a fire...."

"He had a fire, all right," rejoined Hodge briefly.

"Not a false alarm then," said someone else.

"Lost his eyebrows and his greenhouse," said the part-time fireman succinctly.

"All burns are carelessness," pronounced Gordon Briggs with a sanctimoniousness that must have lost him a lot of friends.

"What about the singeing of the beard of the King of Spain," cut in a mischievous walker, one of the few who weren't overawed by the schoolmaster.

"That was politics," said Briggs severely.

Leonard Hodge shrugged his shoulders. "I wouldn't know anything about the King of Spain but I rekon this old boy won't touch paraffin again in a hurry."

The group straggled back through the farmyard towards the kitchen at Pencombe. Detective Inspector Sloan fell into step beside Len Hodge. "I've had a look in Dresham Wood, too," he said to the farmworker.

"Then you've been wasting your time," said Hodge, apparently unperturbed. "Crows wouldn't go into a wood for their pickings. Too dangerous for them." He waved an arm. "They like open country same as this."

Sloan looked up. As if to prove Hodge's point, there were several crows wheeling about overhead.

"Always around the farmyard, they are," said Hodge.

Sloan nodded. That was only natural.

"Plenty of pickings, you see," said Hodge gruffly.

"Of course," agreed Sloan. In the old ballad the new-slain knight had lain out of sight behind an old turfed bank. All such likely places on four farms had now been examined without success. Sloan braced his shoulders. They would just have to go on and look at the unlikely places then. He looked round the farmyard. George Mellot had come out of the back door of the farmhouse and was standing on the doorstep watching him approach. The crows still wheeled overhead. . . .

Sloan halted and said abruptly to Len Hodge, "Where do you keep your ladders?"

"In the barn."

"Show me."

Instead of advancing towards George Mellot the policeman wheeled away from the direction of the back door, and turned into the barn. There was an assortment of ladders stacked against the wall. Sloan pointed to the longest and said to Hodge, "Give me a hand with that one, will you?"

"Sure." Len Hodge lifted his end with consummate ease. "Where do you want it?"

"We'll try the shed first."

Hodge obligingly propped the ladder up against the shed wall. Sloan shinnied up it, conscious of George Mellot's motionless figure on the back doorstep. One quick glance from the right level assured him that there was nothing lying in between the ridges of the roof of the shed. He descended and looked round the farmyard.

"Now the barn, please," said Sloan quietly.

Hodge helped him to carry the ladder back across the farmyard. George Mellot still hadn't moved but out of the corner of his eye Sloan saw Meg Mellot had come forward to the kitchen window. Her white, anxious face was right up against the pane as she watched his every move.

"I want the ladder against the gulley," Sloan said to Hodge, who obediently swung it up without apparent effort and then stood well back in a detached way as if to disassociate himself from the action.

The moment before Sloan set foot on the bottom rung of the ladder remained one etched on his mind as a frozen section of time. There were all the elements of a *tableau vivant* about it—an exhibition of individuals placing themselves in striking attitudes so as to imitate statues. In fact it was the immobility of those watching him that struck Sloan most forcibly. It was as if all three had been fashioned from alabaster.

It was a higher climb to the top of the precast-concrete barn than it had been to the shed roof. When his eyes drew level with the roof-line Detective Inspector Sloan looked along the gutter which lay between the two ridges of the roof.

This time there was something there to see.

EIGHT

•

Lighten our darkness

"And about time, too, Sloan," trumpeted Superintendent Leeyes churlishly down the telephone. "You've had all day."

"Yes, sir." This was undeniable.

"Well? Go on, man...."

"There are more human remains lying on the roof of the barn here at Pencombe Farm," reported Sloan with concision. He was standing in George Mellot's office where the window—like that of the kitchen—gave out onto the farmyard. Detective Constable Crosby was standing on guard at the bottom of the ladder that still stood against the side of the barn but no one was showing the least inclination to go up it.

Superintendent Leeyes grunted.

"It—the skeleton, that is," carried on Sloan, "is lying between the two ridges of the barn roof." There was probably a technical term for the gulley at the bottom of the two slopes—more of a gutter, really—but Sloan did not know what it was. "There's a sort of drain there but it's not quite blocking it."

"That accounts for the damp, I suppose," growled Leeyes. "Dr. Dabbe said he thought the finger had come from somewhere damp, didn't he?"

"Yes, sir," said Sloan, adding, "The doctor's on his way over here now." He paused and then went on significantly, "And so are Dyson and Williams."

Dyson and Williams were the Calleshire force's police photographers.

"Oh, they are, are they?" commented Leeyes trenchantly.

"Yes, sir."

"That means," said Leeyes heavily, "that you've found something more than bones, doesn't it, Sloan?"

"It's more of a case, sir," said the detective inspector, "of not finding something."

Leeyes grunted again. "Like what?"

"There is most of the rest of a human skeleton up there," said Sloan, choosing his words with care.

"Most?" queried Leeyes sharply. "What do you mean?"

"Not all of it."

"Hrrmph," said Leeyes. "So the crows have had a bit more than fingers, have they, then?"

"It's not that, sir," replied Sloan.

"Well," demanded Leeyes peremptorily, "what is it then?"

"There are other fingers missing, too, of course," prevaricated Sloan.

"Naturally," said Leeyes, "but—"

"But," he said apologetically, "I'm afraid the head's not there either."

"What!" exploded Superintendent Leeyes down the telephone.

"It's gone," said Sloan simply.

"But—"

"There's no head there, sir." Strictly speaking, he supposed, he should have used the word "skull."

"A crow," pronounced Leeyes weightily, "couldn't have taken the head away."

"No, sir." That much was self-evident.

"So, Sloan, either someone's been up there since for it—"

"Yes, sir."

"Or," concluded Leeyes flatly, "we're dealing with someone who put a headless corpse up there."

"Exactly, sir."

"You know what that means, Sloan, don't you?"

"Yes, sir," he said. "Murder."

"In either case," said Leeyes.

"Almost certainly," agreed Sloan.

"Why has the head gone?" asked Leeyes after a pause for consideration. "Do you know that, Sloan?"

"There are two reasons that I can think of, sir." It had been the question that had dominated Sloan's own thoughts as he had slowly climbed down the ladder and gone indoors to the telephone.

"Go on."

"Either it reveals the cause of death—"

"A bullet would tell us quite a lot," mused Leeyes, "wouldn't it?"

"It would, sir."

"Ballistics have come on a lot since I was on the beat."

Sloan coughed. "Even a fractured skull would put us in the picture a bit more."

"Hankering after our old friend the blunt instrument, are you, eh, Sloan?"

"Perhaps, sir." Something had killed whoever it was who was lying up there. There was at least no doubt about that. He paused and then said, "There's another reason, though, why the head might have gone, sir."

"Well?"

"A head will most likely have had teeth in it," said Sloan succinctly. Forensic odontology had come on quite as much as the science of ballistics.

"Identification."

"Yes, sir," said Sloan, clearing his throat. "It's going to be quite a problem."

Leeyes grunted. "There must be clues now you've got something to go on."

"As far as I can make out," rejoined Sloan obliquely, "there were no clothes up there with the bones either."

"Naked and dead?" said Leeyes lugubriously.

"Just so, sir."

The superintendent suddenly became very brisk. "Keep me in the picture, Sloan, won't you? This is all very interesting."

"This is all very interesting, Sloan," echoed Dr. Dabbe not very long afterwards. He, too, had now climbed to the top of the ladder propped up against the barn and looked along the roof.

"Yes, Doctor," replied Sloan. Like the superintendent, Dr. Dabbe was able to take a detached view. Sloan couldn't.

"Not so much a body as *disjecta membra*," observed the pathologist.

"Enough for a proper inquest, though?" enquired Sloan. He didn't know what *disjecta membra* were.

"Lord bless you, yes."

"That's something," said Sloan. Invoking the due processes of the law relating to the dead with only a finger to show had a faintly Gilbertian ring about it.

"I'll need a much closer look, of course," said Dr. Dabbe.

"I'm having a scaffolding platform brought out from Berebury." It had only just struck Sloan as odd that the name of the scene of the direst penalty that the law could exact had declined into a mere builders' aid.

"You'll have noticed, Sloan, that the body up there lacks the Yorick touch."

"The head's not there," agreed Sloan more prosaically.

"Alas, poor Yorick," said Dr. Dabbe breezily. "I wonder where it's got to."

"So do I," said Sloan feelingly.

"I'm not promising anything, mind you, Sloan, but with a closer look at the body I might be able to tell you at what stage the head came off."

"That would help," said Sloan moderately.

"And how it came off."

"So would that," said Sloan.

"Haven't seen a true decapitation in years," mused the pathologist.

Detective Inspector Sloan had never seen one. He resolved to be more grateful for small mercies in future.

"Pity's the head's gone, all the same," said Dr. Dabbe regretfully. "So few people are completely edentulous these days that you could have counted on there being teeth."

"Heads are useful," agreed Sloan gravely.

"And should be kept," said the pathologist. "Especially when all about you are losing theirs and blaming it on you." He jerked his head. "You know your Kipling, I take it, Sloan?"

"Yes, Doctor." Now there was a poet that man and boy—and policeman—could understand, though there were those who reckoned that his poem "If" had done them more harm than good. Unrealistic goals led a man to think less of himself when he didn't reach them, that's what the psychologists said when they went on about under- and overachievers. The empire builders, of course, hadn't concerned themselves with the nonachievers—hadn't considered failure as a tenable proposition. . . .

"There's something else that it appears not to have got," observed Dr. Dabbe colloquially.

It was another poem that came into Sloan's mind then. It was called "The Naming of Parts." Rudyard Kipling hadn't lived to write about that war: the war in which they had the naming of parts. It had been Henry Reed who had caught the flavour of those later times with what a man did not have.

"Yes, Doctor," he said aloud, coming back to the present. "I know."

"Like the Emperor," said the pathologist jovially, "it hasn't got any clothes. Did you notice that, Sloan?"

"I did." Sloan didn't know about emperors. He did know

about detection. "It's going to make identification even more difficult," he said.

"It is," agreed the pathologist, rubbing his chin. "On the other hand, Sloan, it did make something else a great deal easier."

Sloan looked up curiously. "What was that?"

Dabbe grinned. "The Little Red Riding Hood touch."

"Pardon, Doctor?"

"All the better to be eaten by crows, Sloan, that's what."

Sloan nodded his comprehension and tightened his lips. It wasn't a happy thought that someone had worked this out. There was a calculation about this crime that betokened a really determined mind scheming away.

"A proper invitation to *corvus corone Linn* to dine is having no clothes," remarked Dr. Dabbe thoughtfully.

"There's nothing," said Sloan, waving a hand in the direction of the barn roof, "at all accidental about any of this."

"On the contrary," agreed the pathologist briskly. "Naked, headless corpses do not in my experience often get themselves onto the roofs of barns."

"And as hiding-places go," observed Sloan judiciously, "it is difficult to think of a better one."

"A grave always shows," pronounced the pathologist.

"He might not have been found," said Sloan, "for years and years." He knew there were mathematical formulae where time and distance were locked together. No one had yet put a name or symbol to the ratio, but time and crime were inextricably interwoven, too. The importance of justice seemed to vary in inverse proportion to the distance of the crime from the time it was brought to book.

There was a subject for study by someone clever, if you like. Sloan had noticed before now that the punishment of an old crime had none of the passion attached to the solving of a new one, fresh in the collective consciousness. An earlier generation of crime-prevention officers had even used the expression "hot pursuit" for newly committed crime with a special meaning all of its own.

"He might not have been found," nodded Dabbe, "except for a crow and a finger."

"Quite so, Doctor." But for a nail a battle had been lost, hadn't it?

"The rest of him mightn't have been noticed for a long time," said Dabbe, giving the barn a critical look. "This building is almost new. It wouldn't have wanted maintenance or painting for years."

Even barns that did need maintenance didn't get it from a lot of the farmers that Sloan knew.

"I reckon, Sloan," continued the pathologist cheerfully, "that you're dealing with someone who had very nearly solved the eternal problem of all murderers—the disposal of the victim."

"That's a great comfort, that is," said Sloan bitterly. It was all very well for Dr. Dabbe to be looking on the bright side. All he had to deal with was the body and the court. He, Sloan, had to tangle with real live villains as well. And clever ones at that, it seemed.

"There's another nice touch about the barn roof as a hiding-place as well," went on Dr. Dabbe, unperturbed.

"What's that?" asked Sloan. It had taken more than brains to think of the barn roof. It had taken imagination too. They were a dangerous combination.

"Sometimes with murder," said the pathologist, "time is of the essence."

"Popping him up there wouldn't have taken all that long," agreed Sloan thoughtfully.

"Although it would have been a bit of a struggle." Dr. Dabbe stroked his chin. "I'll be able to tell you presently if the deceased was a big man."

"However difficult it was to get him up there," rejoined Sloan energetically, "I'll bet it was easier than burying a body in a hurry."

"In some ways, Sloan, it was better, too."

"Better?"

"For the murderer."

"Ah." It was as well to know whose outlook you were considering.

"I don't know if you've ever tried it, Sloan, but six feet of earth takes a fair bit of digging."

"Yes, Doctor, I know." The growing of roses called for quite a lot of spadework.

The doctor raised his nose in the air for all the world like a pointer scenting something. "And one usual objection doesn't apply here."

"What's that, Doctor?"

"Mephitis."

Sloan hunched his shoulders. There was a medical word

whose meaning he did remember. "The smell of the dead," he said.

"If there had been one," said the pathologist, "and there would, nobody would have noticed it here in the middle of a farmyard."

"True." Some person or persons unknown had clearly been very clever indeed, he decided.

"Anyway, Sloan, burial doesn't offer everything."

"No, Doctor?" Whose point of view was the doctor speaking from now?

"Sometimes," murmured Dr. Dabbe reflectively, "burial preserves."

"The Pharaohs, you mean?"

"Not them." The pathologist dismissed the surviving remains of the representatives of several ancient Egyptian dynasties with the wave of a hand. "They were different."

"Ah."

"But with inhumation burial," said Dr. Dabbe more expansively, "you sometimes get adipocere tissue and so forth."

Tissue of any sort was something else they had not got, thought Sloan. In quantity, anyway. He wasn't sure yet how much they did have and wasn't looking forward to finding out.

"Adipocere tissue can help," said Dr. Dabbe.

"I'm sure it can," said Sloan warmly. There was no doubt whose side the doctor was speaking for now.

"With burial, of course," said the doctor, "you have less chance of concealing identity."

"And of removing clues to the cause of death," said Sloan sombrely.

"That, too," agreed the pathologist. "As soon as this scaffolding tower that you've promised arrives, and you let the dog get a proper look at the rabbit, Sloan, I'll tackle your two problems for you."

"Two?" echoed Sloan. He didn't know how on earth the doctor had managed to reduce his problems to only two.

"Identity and cause of death," said Dr. Dabbe neatly. "Those are the things you want to know, Sloan, aren't they?"

"You won't be wanting us any more today, Inspector, will you?" The leader of the Berebury Country Footpaths Society stood squarely in front of Detective Inspector Sloan, knapsack in hand.

"I suppose not, Mr. Briggs," he replied.

The whole atmosphere in the farm kitchen at Pencombe had been changed by the finding of the skeleton. Talk had dried to a trickle and the faintly convivial mood associated with tea-time after a day's walking in the open air had evaporated. It had been succeeded by one of strain and slightly forced conversational exchanges. As if by common consent not one of these present was anywhere near the window which looked out onto the farmyard. Wendy Lamport, standing at the sink and washing up as if her life depended on it, resolutely kept her head down. Mrs. Mellot, concerned and flustered, was drying up cups and saucers at speed.

"We can be going then," said Briggs.

Sloan nodded.

"Now that you've found what you were looking for."

"Yes," said Sloan.

"And we can't do anything more for you anyway, can we?" Gordon Briggs still made no move to go.

"Not at this stage," said Sloan.

Briggs looked up sharply. "What do you mean?"

"There'll be an inquest," said Sloan. "You'll be wanted then."

"Of course," said Briggs quickly.

"That'll come later." An inquest opened and adjourned would be all that the police could ask for from Her Majesty's Coroner for the County of Calleshire. "You'll be told when and where—"

They were interrupted by the sound of breaking china.

A cup had slipped from Meg Mellot's fingers and lay smashed and broken into a dozen pieces on the floor.

"It doesn't matter," she said rather breathlessly into the silence which the sudden noise had brought about. "It doesn't matter at all. I'll get a dustpan and brush."

As abruptly as it had begun the silence ended: all at once everyone started talking again.

"It was there all the time, then, Inspector." Gordon Briggs had spoken about going but in fact continued to stand where he was, unwilling to abandon the subject. "What you were looking for—"

"We think so." Sloan was conscious of some of the other walkers stirring uneasily in the background, clearly anxious to be on their way. Like bit players in life's drama they had acted their parts and were ready to move off-stage. He was equally aware though that there were others who wanted to stay. Although patently no longer required by the action, so to speak, something held them there, fascinated.

"Lying on the roof," Briggs said, underlining the strangeness.

"Yes," said Sloan. Was this how Rosencrantz and Guildenstern had felt? he wondered. After all, they, too, in the beginning had been unwittingly caught up in events not of their choosing.

"If you're sure that we can't do anything to help, Inspector," murmured Briggs. Rosencrantz and Guildenstern had also gone off-stage reluctantly, hadn't they?

"Quite sure," replied Sloan more firmly than he had intended. If he remembered rightly from his school-days Rosencrantz and Guildenstern had been a little uncertain of their roles as well.

"In that case," said Briggs reluctantly, "we'll be on our way then."

In Sloan's school's third form's memorable production of *Hamlet, Prince of Denmark* Rosencrantz had fallen over his own feet as he moved off-stage.

Or had it been Guildenstern?

"Very well," said Sloan. With Rosencrantz and Guildenstern the action had continued somewhere else too.

"Nothing to stay for really, is there, Inspector?"

"Not now."

"Right, then," said Briggs. Half turn to go yet turning stay . . . No, that had been another poet altogether.

"You'll be having a proper letter," Sloan promised him, "thanking your society for all its help."

"When the dust has settled a bit, eh?" said Briggs.

"When our investigations are complete," said Sloan formally.

"You've hardly started, have you?" said the schoolmaster. "I can see that."

"Let us say," Sloan answered him grandly, conscious now that he was quoting the great, "that we've reached the end of the beginning."

NINE

•

The pestilence that walketh in darkness

"Paul, is that you?" The telephone bell had rung at Upper-combe Farm and had been answered with alacrity. "This is Andrina."

"Hullo," he said guardedly.

"Have you heard?"

"Yes," replied Paul Hucham soberly. "George rang me."

"He rang me too," she said in a small voice.

"He told me he was going to," said Hucham, conscious of sounding stifled.

"You might have let me know first," said Andrina Ritchie lightly. "Before he did. It would have been a little less of a shock."

"I did think about that," explained Hucham truthfully, "but George was dead set on telling everyone himself. You know how he feels about being a good neighbour. He'd already rung old Sam before he rang me."

"All the same," she said, "it was a bit of a surprise."

Hucham responded to that with something approaching fervour. "You can say that again."

"Did he say," she asked, "that they think it must be some stranger?"

"No," said Hucham, "now that I come to think about it, he didn't say that."

"That's funny," said Andrina Ritchie. "I should have thought he would have done."

"It didn't sound," said Paul Hucham consideringly, "as if he'd had time to do a lot of thinking."

She changed the subject a little. "You can see Pencombe from where you are, can't you?"

"If I look." Paul Hucham picked up the telephone receiver and shifted his position slightly so that he could see out of the nearest window. The view gave out over the valley.

"Can't you tell what's going on there?" There was more than a little impatience in Andrina Ritchie's voice.

"Not really."

"You must be able to see something—"

"Just that there's a lot of activity down there."

"What sort of activity?"

"Well, for one thing I can see that there are a lot of jam sandwiches about."

"Jam sandwiches? Are you mad?"

"White police cars with red stripes round them."

Mrs. Andrina Ritchie was not amused. "This isn't the best time to be funny, Paul."

"No use getting strung up," he said. "That never does any good."

"I must say George Mellot sounded very uptight."

"Who wouldn't?" asked the sheep-farmer reasonably. "Having a skeleton found in your backyard is enough to throw any man."

"Don't!"

"Well, it's true."

"I suppose so. And to think," she said, "that it might have lain up there for years and years without being found."

"So it might," he agreed.

"George told me that they'd got police everywhere."

"Bound to have," opined the sheep-farmer with calculated casualness. "It's only natural in the circumstances."

"That's all very well but—"

"I wouldn't have expected anything else myself," he said with a touch of firmness.

"I was thinking," said Andrina Ritchie with a fine show of indirectness, "of going over to Pencombe to ask if I might borrow their fork-lift tractor for tomorrow morning. Jenkins could use it to lift some bales."

"I shouldn't do that if I were you," said Hucham carefully. "For all you know Len Hodge may be needing it too. Besides, they'll have quite enough to be thinking about as it is without your turning up there."

"Perhaps you're right."

"I know I am," said Paul Hucham confidently. "Added to which," he went on smoothly, "I don't suppose for one moment that the police will let anyone move anything into or out of that farmyard from now on."

She shuddered. "I hadn't thought about that."

"Mind how you go," adjured Detective Constable Crosby. "I've been in some funny places in my time," responded

Dyson, the police photographer, "but this is as daft as any of them."

"You'll be all right if you hold on," said Crosby.

"It's all right for you," rejoined the photographer with spirit. "You don't have to carry anything."

This was true. Dyson, on the other hand, was hung about with quite as much equipment as Don Quixote's attendant, Sancho Panza.

"Don't let go of the ladder, that's all," said Crosby.

"And how do you suppose I take photographs if I'm holding on to a ladder? With my teeth?"

"If you don't hold on to the ladder," promised Crosby flatly, "you'll fall off."

"And if I do," responded Dyson, "I suppose the thing to do is to look out for the view on my left as I fall?"

"All you'll see if you do that is—"

"I can guess," said the photographer bitterly. "A midden."

"You said it," said Crosby.

"I can smell it from here." Dyson advanced towards the ladder against the scaffolding tower. "It doesn't look very safe to me."

"It isn't," said Crosby laconically.

"All in the cause of duty, I suppose. You can put that on my tombstone. Make a nice epitaph. Come along, Williams. . . ." Williams was his assistant. "Got the tripod all right? I expect you want me to go first. . . ."

This remark was greeted with the silence that lawyers say amounts to consent and Dyson approached the ladder that was propped up against a hastily erected scaffolding tower designed to bring the investigators level with the skeleton.

"Onward, ever onward, go," declared Dyson, taking the first step up the ladder. It shook visibly. "Hold it, man. Don't just stand there."

"I am holding it," retorted Crosby in injured tones. "It's shaking because there isn't any firm ground for it to stand on."

"That's a great comfort, I must say," called Dyson over his shoulder. "No flowers, by the way, if I should die on duty. Just send the money."

"It won't do you any good where you're going," said Crosby.

"Are you quite sure about that, old man? I thought money and hell were as inextricably mixed as money and living. It's the other place where they won't be bothering with trifles

like money any more. . . ." Dyson's head suddenly drew level
with the top of the scaffolding platform and the bottom of the
barn roof. He looked along the gulley at the skeleton and
called down, "I say, this chap's a bit beyond aid, isn't he?"

"Yes," said Crosby simply.

"Talk about something nasty in the woodshed," said Dyson,
sucking his teeth sharply. "This is a lot worse than that."

"It is," agreed Crosby.

"Not nice at all." Dyson had clambered from the top of the
ladder onto the scaffolding platform and advanced to the edge
of the roof. He called down, "You'd better come up, too,
Williams. We'll need that tripod."

"Hand shaking, then?" enquired Crosby pleasantly. "Or
just lonely up there?"

"You know me," rejoined Dyson. "Nervous as a young filly."

Williams started to climb the ladder. Dyson had taken his
first picture well before the other man got to the top. "The
trouble is," he called down, "unless I can get up on to one of
these ridges, any view I take is going to be a bit too
foreshortened for comfort."

"You can't go onto the ridge," called back Crosby. "Not
yet."

"In that case," said Dyson philosophically, "the view will
just have to be foreshortened."

"No one is to go on the roof until it's been examined
properly." The technical problems of professional photographers didn't trouble the detective constable unduly but orders were, in any case, orders. "There may be some footprints up there."

"I'll photograph them too," said Dyson helpfully, "if I can
find any."

"If you ask me," said Crosby, "it's been too dry."

"Someone must have stood up there on the roof to drag
him far enough along the valley between the ridges to be out
of sight," said Dyson.

"We know that," responded Crosby regally.

"The question is, then, did they leave any traces?" said the
police photographer.

"Everything leaves traces," the detective constable chanted
Edmund Locard's Principle of Interchange. "Whether there's
anything to photograph is a different matter."

Dyson raised his camera again and took a number of shots
of the skeleton in quick succession from different angles.

"If you step back any farther," forecast Crosby from below, "Williams here will be photographing you instead of him, whoever he is."

"It would be a good way to go, wouldn't it?" called back the photographer. "You must admit, Crosby, that this chap up here, whatever he's called, hasn't a care in the world any longer."

"Which is more than can be said for the rest of us," interposed Williams, arriving rather breathlessly on the platform beside Dyson. "Here's the tripod."

"And there's the subject," said Dyson tersely.

"Blimey O'Riley!" exclaimed Williams.

"Exactly," said Crosby.

"Do you know anything about him?" called down Dyson.

"Just the one thing," replied Detective Constable Crosby sedulously.

"What's that?"

"He's got no head for heights," and the constable, putting his foot on the bottom rung of the ladder.

George Mellot and his employee, Leonard Hodge, were not in the farm kitchen with the members of the Berebury Country Footpaths Society. They were standing together outside in the farmyard watching the police photographers at work on the barn roof. The policemen who had helped to make up the search-party had been detailed to examine the farm buildings and were now scouring the ground like so many human vacuum cleaners. George Mellot bore the sight of them poking into every nook and cranny of Pencombe Farm as dispassionately as he could. Len Hodge, though, was visibly upset.

"It's a sight worse than that scare we had last year, isn't it, gov'nor?" he said to his employer.

"What scare, Len?" George Mellot took his mind off the present with an effort. Last year seemed altogether too remote for memory recall just now.

"You remember," said Hodge. "When they wondered if we'd got foot-and-mouth disease at Pencombe."

"Oh, that . . ." At the time George Mellot hadn't been able to envisage a worse disaster than an outbreak of foot-and-mouth disease in the Pencombe herd of Guernsey cows. He could now. Things were different. It was a measure of his present anxiety that he had almost forgotten the earlier one.

"That was nothing," he said. The funny thing was that he meant it, too.

Now.

Hodge hitched his shoulder in the direction of the barn roof. "Who could have guessed that there was anything up there?" he asked.

"No one," said the farmer shortly.

Hodge jerked his thumb upwards to the sky. "And there are always crows in the yard, aren't there?"

"Always," agreed Mellot.

"I must say," sniffed Hodge, "I never took no notice of them myself."

"Neither did I," said Mellot.

Hodge hunched his shoulders. "You sort of get used to them being around somehow."

"Of course you do," the farmer said, adding carefully, "The police aren't saying we should have noticed, Len."

"Yet," emphasized Hodge. "They aren't saying anything yet, are they?"

"True." In fact the silence of the police was one of the things George Mellot was finding most difficult of all. So far they were keeping their own counsel about everything and it was hard to endure.

"It's a bad business, all the same," Hodge said obliquely, "him lying up there and us working down here all the time."

"Doesn't bear too much thinking about," agreed George Mellot in his usual understated way.

Suddenly Hodge looked up and turned abruptly. "Hullo, hullo," he drawled. "Here comes trouble...."

"Ted Mason," said George Mellot. "Back again."

"Where have you been, then, Ted?" said Hodge to the policeman.

"Back home to see if there were any messages," said the village constable.

"For a bite to eat, more like," said Hodge.

Constable Mason looked down at his portly frame. "Well, seeing as I was there and it happened to be there I did have a slice of cake," he said with dignity. "Makes a most acceptable fruit-cake, does the wife."

Hodge sniffed. "Missed all the action, you did."

"So I hear," replied Mason equably.

"It's a gift...."

"It was a very good cake," insisted Mason with the fervour of the fat.

"Some people have all the luck," said Hodge scornfully.

George Mellot stirred. "Does anyone have any idea at all who it is up there?"

"We're pursuing our enquiries," parroted Constable Mason immediately. He then promptly spoilt the whole effect of this noncommittal pronouncement by adding, "Not a clue, Mr. Mellot, really. Have you got any suggestions, Len?"

Hodge shook his head.

"From what I hear," said George Mellot, "whoever's up there is a bit far gone for clues."

"Don't you believe it," said Mason cheerfully. "They're so clever these days they can even tell you what a mummy in a museum died from."

"That's a great help, that is," said Hodge.

"Oh, it'll take time, of course," continued the constable largely. "These things always do."

"What about the evening milking?" asked Hodge.

"It'll take time," repeated Mason, ignoring the tricky question of the evening milking. "We know that but I daresay we'll find out all about it in the end. We usually do."

"Where will you start?" asked the farmer.

"Here." Mason waved an arm in a gesture that encompassed the policemen diligently going over the farmyard as well as the complex that was Pencombe Farm. "Where the evidence is."

"And then?"

"Missing persons," said Mason promptly. "It must be someone who's missing, mustn't it?"

Hodge nodded at the logic of this. "Stands to reason."

"Where do you go from there, though?" persisted George Mellot. "A lot of people go missing."

"Then we go into the logistics, Mr. Mellot." Mason might not be any great shakes at activity but he was perfectly sound on theory.

Hodge looked up suspiciously. "Clever stuff, eh?"

"Logistics isn't clever, Len," said Mason. "It's just working out how a crime was committed in the way it was."

Hodge scowled. "Like, did he fall or was he pushed?"

"That's the general idea," said Mason. "And when we've worked that out," he added neatly, "then we go on to other things."

"What other things?" demanded Hodge truculently.

"Like how did he get up there?" said Mason steadily.

A silence fell upon the little group. As if motivated by mesmerism all three looked upwards to the barn roof.

"That sometimes tells you quite a lot," remarked Mason.

Neither of the other two spoke.

"Not everyone," continued Mason conversationally, "could get a body up on to a roof, could they? Women and children, for instance..."

That wrung an unwilling assent from both his listeners.

"Take a fair bit of doing," admitted Hodge grudgingly.

"It would sort out the men from the boys," agreed George Mellot.

"Mind you," went on Constable Mason, "there's always the easy way, isn't there?"

"What do you mean by that?" asked Mellot.

The policeman let his gaze drift towards the fork-lift tractor standing by the barn. "That would get it a good part of the way up, wouldn't it? If not to the very top..."

"So it would," said George Mellot in tones utterly devoid of emphasis.

"Quite surprising really," observed Mason, "that neither of you happened to mention it."

Hodge started involuntarily. "So that's why—" He stopped as suddenly as he had begun.

Both men turned to him.

"So that's why what, Len?" asked Mason silkily.

"Nothing," said Hodge, clamping his jaws together and falling silent.

"You were going to say something," said Mason.

"No I wasn't," declared Hodge belligerently. "I wasn't going to say nothing and you can't say I was, Ted Mason."

TEN

•

The deeds of darkness

Psychologists insist that every normal human being needs someone who is known as a speech friend. It is with this speech friend that the details of the small happenings of daily life are regularly exchanged. In the manner of their kind these same psychologists do not indicate whether this role is always filled by a spouse, but there was no doubt about that in the case of Sam Bailey.

The news of the finding of the skeleton had come to Lowercombe Farm earlier, but Sam Bailey hadn't been able to share it with his wife, Maggie, because he couldn't find her. There being nothing more irritating than being the possessor of interesting news and yet not being able to impart that news to anyone, the old farmer was in a fine state of indignation by the time he did meet her. She was standing in the farmhouse hall with a bunch of flowers in her arms.

"Where have you been?" he said crossly. "I've been looking for you everywhere."

A lesser woman might have referred to the garden. A more distant relation might have even waved the flowers at him. Elsie Bailey, however, had been married to him for the best part of forty years.

"What's wrong?" she asked practically instead.

"The police."

Her head came up sharply. "What about them?"

"They've found what they were looking for."

"Oh." Her anxiety palpably subsided.

"George Mellot rang to tell us." He added another grievance. "I thought you'd come in when the telephone rang. You know I don't like answering it."

"Poor soul." She laid the flowers down on the hall table. "It can't be anyone we know, Sam, can it?"

He shook his grizzled head. "That's one thing to be thankful for. What do you want with those flowers anyway, Elsie? There are flowers everywhere already."

"Poor George and Meg," she said. "It can't be very nice for them. And they've had a lot of extra worry lately anyway what with one thing and another."

"At least it wasn't foot-and-mouth in the end."

"A herd isn't everything, Sam."

"Troubles never come on their own," said Bailey. That made him remember something else that had caused him to feel deprived. "That beef we had today—"

"Sam, there was nothing wrong with that beef. It was the best that Hubert Wilkinson—"

"I know there wasn't. That's what I mean," he said indignantly. "I thought it would be nice to have it cold with pickle tonight and I couldn't find it in the larder."

"I've made you a pie for supper. You like pie."

He wasn't listening. "And another thing, Elsie."

"What?" she enquired patiently.

"My raincoat. I can't find it."

"I expect you've put it somewhere and forgotten where," she said tranquilly. "It's not raining, anyway."

"It wasn't there when I got back from church."

"By the way," she said obliquely, "I thought you read the lesson very well this morning. The rector said so too."

"Huh!" snorted Bailey. "He wants the churchyard mowing."

"You are a churchwarden," pointed out his wife.

"What's that got to do with it?"

"And you have got a gang mower."

"It's been the same for forty years," he grumbled. "Every June."

"Grass grows every year," said his wife.

"Let him ask me, then," growled Bailey.

"You've done it every year."

"He's only got to ask," insisted the old man, "and I'll send someone down to do it."

"And your father before you," she said. "Baileys from Lowercombe have always kept the churchyard mown."

"Now don't you start on that, Elsie. The rector can have his churchyard cut the minute he asks me."

"On bended knee?" she enquired ironically.

"I've got my pride and he's got his."

"Oh, Sam," she said softly, "you are a stiff-necked old fool and well you know it."

*　　　*　　　*

George Mellot left the farmyard and went indoors with the
slow heavy tread of a worried man. His wife had been
standing by the window watching him approach but she did
not turn round when he came into the kitchen. Instead she
kept her back towards him as if afraid to meet his eye.

"Len knows something," he said without preamble.

"I wondered," she said.

"About the fork-lift tractor," said Mellot flatly.

"I noticed that he'd suddenly gone all quiet," she said.

"Ted Mason spotted it, too," said Mellot. "About the fork-
lift tractor, I mean."

She did turn to face him then. "It's not like Len to be so
quiet."

"Not that Mason could have missed it." Mellot was pursuing his own gloomy line of thought. "Len got all uptight as
soon as Mason even mentioned the fork-lift tractor, let alone
took a proper look at it."

"It must be obvious, mustn't it"—she swallowed visibly—
"that that's what got . . . it . . . up there."

"There's nothing else around," agreed the farmer grimly,
"that would have done the job half so well."

"Don't!"

"Any policeman could see that with half an eye. There's no
use pretending—"

"Len did work for your father, too, when he was a boy,"
said Meg with seeming irrelevance. "Didn't he? And so did
his father."

"Oh, he won't say anything," said Mellot confidently. "Not
Len. I'm pretty sure about that."

"That's all very well but it's not going to make a lot of
difference to the police, is it?" responded Mrs. Mellot. "They'll
just go on until they find out."

Her husband sat down at the kitchen table and sunk his
head down into his hands like an old, old man. "I know."

"And there's another thing I've thought of," said Meg with
lowered eyes.

"What's that?"

"Not everyone can work one of those machines, can they?"

"No."

"It's not like driving a car. You need to know how. There
are levers and things," she said. "I've seen them."

"The police will work that out, too," he said wearily. "They
aren't fools."

"That will narrow down who can have used it."

"That's what's worrying me."

"And Len—"

"I must say," remarked Mellot, "that Len has been a bit difficult this past week or two."

"Longer."

He shrugged his shoulders. "You notice these things and I don't."

"He's had something on his mind, anyway," she said. "I could tell that much from talking to him."

"I've never known him to keep out of my way so much," agreed Mellot. "I haven't been able to find him half the time."

"I would say," said Meg slowly, "that it was since that day he came to work with a black eye. Do you remember? And he wouldn't say what had happened. He was bruised, too."

Mellot lifted his head in slow wonderment. "I'd forgotten all about that."

"Oh, George, do you think—" She stopped.

"That was about a month ago, wasn't it?"

She nodded. "It was a Monday morning when he came to work looking like a prize-fighter. I do remember that."

With leaden, unwilling movements her husband slowly swivelled round to peer at the calendar hanging on the kitchen wall. "A Monday, did you say?" he echoed hollowly. "About four weeks ago—"

"The beginning of the month." She followed his gaze as if mesmerized.

He turned quickly away from the calendar and sat back at the table again, his hands covering his eyes. "June the fifth, that would have been. Oh, dear, oh, dear . . ."

"What will the police do next?" asked Meg Mellot tremulously.

"They want to talk to me." With the hesitation of one conveying unwelcome news George Mellot added, "And they've asked for Tom's address."

Detective Inspector Sloan went indoors to the telephone at Pencombe Farm unwillingly. The message had been that Superintendent Leeyes was on the line from Berebury asking for a progress report.

"The situation, sir," said Sloan, stressing the word slightly and not mentioning progress at all, "is that the doctor is up there now with the remains and that the farmyard is being searched very carefully as quickly as possible."

"Quickly?" Leeyes pronounced. "I don't like rushed jobs, Sloan."

"There's a herd of cows waiting to be got into their milking parlour, sir." If Sloan could have hung the telephone receiver out of the window the Superintendent would have been able to hear the mournful sound of lowing wafting across the farmyard in eerie confirmation of this fact.

"Tricky," agreed Leeyes immediately.

"It's long past their milking time as it is," said Sloan. They both knew that if he kept the cows out of the milking shed and the court ever got to hear about it, the prosecution case would be as good as lost.

Leeyes grunted. "It's always difficult with animals." It was a lesson learned hard and early in the police force. Every chief constable had had to deal with lost dogs in his day. And then it wasn't so much a case of every dog having its day as every day having its dog. . . .

"Always," agreed Sloan fervently. There had only been one thing worse than lost dogs and that was escaped budgerigars. Little old ladies seemed to think that these were easier to capture than professional criminals and they weren't. There was no doubt, though, that animals ranked over men in sentiment as far as the great British public was concerned. Always over dead men. And especially over very dead men.

"So, Sloan . . ."

"So, sir, we're going over the farmyard first." It wasn't that Sloan was an animal lover: rather that he was a realist. There wasn't a jury in the United Kingdom that would have agreed to the theoretical requirements of justice being subverted to the actual needs of the animal kingdom.

"And then?"

"We'll tackle the roof. We think, sir," he added cautiously, "that we know how the body was got up there."

"Ha!"

"There is a fork-lift tractor in the yard."

He was answered with an unexpected witticism. "A means to an end, eh, Sloan?"

"Quite so," he said, dutifully acknowledging this. He cleared his throat. "There is a farmworker here who gives the impression of knowing more than he's telling us. Mason is sure about that."

Leeyes grunted.

"Moreover," continued Sloan, "he's the man who about a

month ago had a fight with a mysterious stranger in the pub here in Great Rooden."

"Nonsense," countered his superior officer robustly. "You don't get mysterious strangers in villages. You should know that, Sloan. Everybody knows everybody."

"Yes, sir." Sloan accepted the rebuke meekly. "I'll remember that."

"And another thing..."

"Sir?"

"People don't fight people they don't know," said Leeyes profoundly.

"No, sir."

"There's no point in it."

Sloan rephrased what he had said. "He had a fight with a man nobody's telling us about."

"That's better."

"Tomorrow, sir," Sloan forged on. Even though today had been endless, tomorrow would come. "Tomorrow I'd like the search-party back."

"One body not enough, then?"

"To search Dresham Wood," said Sloan steadily.

"Ah!" The superintendent's response came alertly down the telephone line.

"There's something in there, sir, I'm sure, but I don't know what." At Cold Comfort Farm there had been something in the woodshed but here at Great Rooden whatever it was was in the wood. Sloan was sure about that. At Cold Comfort Farm it had been something nasty. It might well be something nasty in the wood here. Only a proper search would tell.

"Tomorrow," observed Leeyes gloomily, "may be too late."

Sloan's mother was a great reader of the Bible and from time to time Sloan was glad about this. A working knowledge of how helpful Job's comforters had been to Job had stood Sloan in good stead when functioning with the superintendent. He didn't argue. Instead he said, "I've put out a general call for Martin Ritchie of Stanestede. It would be nice to cross him off our list."

"One less missing man to be bothering about," agreed Leeyes.

"The timing's right for it to be him," Sloan reminded the superintendent.

"It is for Ivor Harbeton, too," pointed out Leeyes. "Those papers about him should have got to you by now."

"And," persisted Sloan, "the timing's right for whoever it was that Hodge had a fight with. That was at the beginning of June, too."

"We mustn't forget him," said Leeyes. "The...ah...the third man, you might say."

"Yes, sir," agreed Sloan. The superintendent's responses were a little dated these days. "Martin Ritchie, Ivor Harbeton and the third man."

"Unless," said Leeyes, "Hodge had a fight with one of the other two—with Harbeton or Ritchie, I mean. Then there would be only two men in the picture, wouldn't there?"

They said, didn't they, that the counting nursery rhymes were the oldest of all. The one that Sloan couldn't get out of his mind was about pigs.

And this little piggy went to market and this little piggy stayed at home....

He couldn't remember what had happened to the third pig.

The parlour at Pencombe Farm wasn't an ideal murder headquarters but Sloan decided that it would do. It was a pleasant, relaxed room with a few pieces of good furniture in evidence: and there was that about the carpet which made Detective Constable Crosby look twice at the state of the soles of his shoes as he came in from the farmyard.

On a rather nice burr walnut table was a bowl of freshly gathered ligtu hybrid alstroemeria and on the windowsill a skilful arrangement of old rose. Detective Inspector Sloan grew roses as a hobby and he cast an appraising eye over them, noting the varieties. He had already seen a good pure white Seagull rambler growing round the front door, and the crimson purple Gallica Tuscany Superb by the gate. This farmer's wife didn't have to devote herself exclusively to the farm: there was time and money at Pencombe to spare and it showed.

Detective Constable Crosby chose the stoutest chair in the room and lowered himself into it with care. "What's the betting, sir," he said, "that we're going to get three monkeys treatment about that skeleton?"

"What's that?" asked Sloan absently. He had opted to sit on a Knole sofa done up in an old-fashioned chintz with contrasting plain sea-green cushions. He began to open the message wallet that the superintendent had had sent over from Berebury Police Station.

"They saw nothing," chanted Crosby, "they heard nothing and—"

"I know, I know," said Sloan morosely. "You don't need to tell me—"

"And they're going to say nothing," finished Crosby triumphantly.

"Maybe." Sloan ran his eye over the sheaf of press cuttings which had been sent by the superintendent. They were all about the disappearance of Ivor Harbeton. "We'll know in a minute. The Mellots are on their way."

Crosby got his notebook out.

"It says here," said Sloan, who had been studying one of the press cuttings in detail, "that Harbeton was a man of medium height. See that Dr. Dabbe is told, will you? And while you're about it, you might check how tall the amorous Martin Ritchie was."

"Yes, sir."

"You can't be too careful in this game." That was one thing that was certain in an uncertain world.

"Shall I see if there's anyone called Beverley missing, too, sir?"

"Who's Beverley?" asked Sloan blankly.

"The girl who Martin Ritchie has gone off with," said Crosby.

"By all means," said Sloan warmly, "although, of course, she may not be missing at all."

"But—"

"She," observed Sloan pithily, "may merely have used the time-honoured phrase 'Come live with me and be my love' and he did."

"Pardon, sir?"

"Nothing," said Sloan. "You go ahead and check." He stopped, struck by a sudden thought. "She may not exist, of course. We have no evidence that she does."

"The letter—"

"The letter was thrown away by the outraged Mrs. Ritchie. 'Cupid,'" quoted Sloan neatly, "'is a knavish lad.'" The poet might have said it first but it was a lesson learned early on the beat.

Crosby made a note in his book

"Ivor Harbeton," said Sloan, waving a piece of newspaper in his hand, "was last seen on Friday, June second."

"Three—no, more than that—four weeks ago," said Crosby, counting them out on his fingers.

"The day that the auditors were due at one of his company's offices," continued Sloan, reading aloud.

"Auditors shouldn't say when they're coming," said Crosby. "They don't with banks, you know, sir. Catches out the teemers and laders a treat."

"It doesn't sound from reading this," responded Sloan mildly, "as if Ivor Harbeton is the sort of man to be bothered about a little thing like fiddling the receipt book."

"June isn't the season, anyway," contributed Crosby. "Not for that. It's more of a Christmas crime."

Sloan nodded. Teeming and lading were common among shaky club treasurers, defalcation reaching its peak during December. Nemesis usually caught up with them in January.

"I rather think," he said drily, "that Ivor Harbeton is in a bigger league than Christmas clubs, risky as they are too."

"Not a petty-cash man," said Crosby.

"High finance," said Sloan, although he wasn't at all sure what the phrase meant. The newspapers had used it more than once. And the word "wheeler-dealer" too, but all the reporting was neatly circumspect. Peccadillo—let alone fraud—wasn't even hinted at. Newspapers were more subtle than that. "He was prominent in City circles," Sloan read aloud from a cutting.

Crosby snorted gently. "And now he's decamped."

"Let us say," replied Sloan with precision, "that nobody quite seems to know exactly where he is."

"Vamoosed," said Crosby, lapsing still further into the vernacular.

"Perhaps," suggested Sloan, waving a hand vaguely in the direction of the farmyard, "he didn't get very far—"

They were interrupted by the arrival of George and Meg Mellot. They advanced unwillingly.

"You said you wanted to see us, Inspector," said the farmer.

"Just one or two questions about the skeleton," began Sloan easily.

"There's not a lot we can tell you," said Mellot.

"We didn't know anything about its being there," supplemented his wife anxiously, her eyes on her husband's face. "Did we, George?"

George Mellot shook his head.

"We shall need some sort of statement to that effect for the coroner," carried on Sloan smoothly. "For the inquest."

"Of course," said George Mellot at once.

It was always surprising, thought Sloan to himself, how reassuring nearly everyone found both mention of the coroner and the invoking of that most ancient of Norman institutions, an inquest.

"Naturally," said Meg Mellot.

However ambivalent their attitude to the police, the great British public saw the coroner as an impartial enquirer: inquests were a time-honoured procedure that could—and did—happen in the best of families. And, thought Sloan, generously giving credit where credit was due, it was amazing how very above the battle the coroner always contrived to appear.

"For instance," Sloan, coming back to the matter at hand, "it would be useful to know if either of you had heard anything strange at any time lately."

Both Mellots immediately shook their heads.

"Not even," said Sloan, "the dog barking without a reason?"

"No," said Mellot.

"Never," said his wife, nervously plucking at her skirt.

"Where does it sleep?" asked Sloan.

"Outside," replied the farmer. "In the yard."

"I see." Sloan paused before he said, "And I take it that you have neither of you seen any unauthorized persons about the farmyard lately?" When he was very small he remembered his mother—no, it must have been his grandmother—teaching him the old song "Hark, hark, the dogs do bark, the beggars are coming to town."

"No," said George Mellot firmly.

All the energy seemed to have gone out of Meg Mellot. She was sitting in the chair with her hands lying loosely clasped together, palms upward, in what the art historians called the Byzantine attitude of sustained sorrow.

Sloan reached out his hand for one of the press cuttings and said, "Does the name Ivor Harbeton convey anything to you, Mr. Mellot?"

He never did get a direct answer to his question.

The detective inspector had hardly asked it before he saw the colour drain out of Meg Mellot's face. She emitted a low moan and subsided onto the parlour floor at his feet in a dead faint.

ELEVEN

•

Your adversary the devil

"I say, Calleshire," chattered the voice on the telephone line, "you do realise that today's a Sunday, don't you?"

"Yes," said Sloan evenly. In the police force you knew not the day nor the hour when you might be working. "Yes, Met, I do."

"City," the voice corrected him with celerity. "Not Met."

"Sorry," said Sloan. That had been a *faux pas* of the first order.

"You're talking to the City Fraud Squad," said the voice. "That's who you wanted, wasn't it?"

"It was," said Sloan. "I'm sorry about its being a Sunday but we've got a bit of a problem down here."

"Speak on."

"Can you tell me anything about a character called Ivor Harbeton?"

"You bet I can." Something approaching a cackle came down the telephone line. "Don't say that he's been operating in your neck of the woods, too?"

"Not operating, exactly," said Sloan obscurely.

"But—"

"But there may be a link." Perhaps, thought Sloan, that was too restrained a way of putting it. Mrs. Meg Mellot had canted over at the mere mention of the man's name. And taken her time to come round.

"You'll be lucky to come off best," said the voice frankly. "Nobody else has that we can see."

"Tell me," invited Sloan. Victims often brought death on themselves. In more ways than one.

"He's clever," said the voice grudgingly. "I give him that."

Sloan was not surprised. The unclever did not as a rule attract the attentions of either the Fraud Squad or the newspapers. The Bench of Magistrates dealt with them and then went home to their wives complaining about the low level of education in the country.

"An entrepreneur," expanded the man in London, "that's what I would call Ivor Harbeton."

It wasn't surprising, thought Sloan, that a nation of shop-
keepers didn't have the right word.

"And," went on the voice drily, "he's nearly always nearly
legal."

"Ah," said Sloan. Those were the difficult cases. Give him a
flagrant breach of the law any day. Justice hanging on a pure
technicality didn't go down well with either judge or jury.
Even less well when hanging had been the operative word.

"Quite ruthless, of course," continued the voice in a detached way.

Ruthlessness was not an endearing characteristic. It might
have been that that had made a victim of Ivor Harbeton. If he
was the victim, that is. Sloan didn't know yet. What he did
know was that Meg Mellot had abruptly fainted at his feet.
And that her husband had gone down on his knees beside
her, imploring her to lie quiet and still until she felt better.

"There's no sentiment in business," carried on his interloc-
utor in the City breezily, "but I would have said Ivor Harbeton
was born without it anyway."

"Anything known?" enquired Sloan. That was police short-
hand for a lot.

"He hasn't got form," replied the voice, "but then generally speaking the villains we deal with in this department don't
have."

In police parlance, though, they were still villains.

"Not until the balloon goes up in a big way, that is," said
the Fraud Squad man.

"And has it with Ivor Harbeton?" asked Sloan.

"Let us say," responded the voice cautiously, "that we
should like to talk to him. Very much indeed. And so would
the people at United Mellemetics."

"United Mellemetics?" Sloan scratched about in his memory.
"They're a big firm in the north, aren't they?"

"They are. For their sins they got taken over in April by
Hobblethwaite Castings—that's one of Harbeton's other
companies—in April this year. With Harbeton as chairman of
the board."

"And they didn't like it?"

"United Mellemetics," replied the voice succinctly, "were
stripped naked of every asset they held. And the money—"

"Yes?" Sloan was always interested in what happened to
money. It was the policeman in him.

"The money was applied to financing the next take-over battle."

"Battle." Sloan echoed the word. The language of war sat as appropriately on the background of business as it did on that of crime.

"Well, if you want to be exact," said the Fraud Squad man astringently, "I should say that rapine and pillage describe what went on at United Mellemetics better, but then I'm old-fashioned myself."

"And then?"

"Then the United Mellemetics auditors went on the war-path."

"And found that there had been sticky fingers in the till?" enquired Sloan colloquially.

"And found themselves unable to reconcile the figures with what was left of the assets," said the other man more technically.

"That's bad." Even Sloan, who did not count himself as numerate, could see that.

"The fixed assets were there all right, but—"

"But the liquid ones had evaporated?" supplemented Sloan. There was even something insubstantial about the very phase. Liquid, indeed!

"Happens all the time," said the voice from the City laconically.

Detective Inspector Sloan of the Calleshire County Constabulary said he could well believe it.

"Take it from me, old man," said the Fraud Squad man, "and keep your money in short-dated government stock. You know exactly where you are then."

"Quite so," replied Sloan noncommittally. Actually he wasn't at all sure that you did know where you were with government. Even chief constables didn't always know. Home secretaries came in different colours. And in different degrees of dampness. Some were wet and some were dry.

"And with short-dated government stock," said the other man, "there's always the date of redemption to look forward to." He made it sound like the Day of Judgement.

"I don't have anything much left over," responded Sloan quickly. "Not with my mortgage." This was not strictly true but money over and above and to spare in the Sloan ménage was apt to be absorbed by purchases from the catalogues of specialist rose growers. He cleared his throat and asked, "Where do you come in with the man Harbeton?"

"The people at United Mellemetics came to us when they discovered the—er—shortfall."

It was funny how malfeasance—like death—attracted euphemisms. Shrinkage was another word that meant more than one might think.

"So we started to make enquiries," carried on the speaker, "and we found that two and two didn't make four either."

"Ah."

"By then, of course, Ivor Harbeton had gone on to his next take-over battle."

"Mellot's Furnishings," said Sloan simply.

"Oh, you know about that, do you?"

"Only what the newspapers say."

"He did it through Conway's Covers, which is another Harbeton company," amplified the Fraud Squad man. "Don't ask me to tell you them all. Proteus isn't in it."

"If we could concentrate on Mellot's Furnishings..."

The man at the other end of the telephone line brightened audibly. "That's easy, Inspector. When all this started Mellot's Furnishings was a well-run company with prime sites in most towns."

"Ripe for plucking." Sloan could see that.

"The ideal victim. Couldn't have been better, in fact. The recipe's quite easy. Take it over, sell the shop sites, lease them back to the company, and use the capital for something else."

It couldn't, thought Detective Inspector C. D. Sloan, first-time home-owner, be as simple as that. The hassle of buying one semi-detached house in suburban Berebury had been bad enough. He said so.

"It is simple," insisted the other man airily. "And perfectly legal. It goes on all the time."

Sloan felt stirred into protest. "It's not the sort of thing to take lying down."

A grim laugh travelled along the telephone line. "Tom Mellot didn't do that, believe you me."

"What did he do, then?"

The man from the Fraud Squad told him.

That was when Detective Constable Crosby materialised at his elbow. "The doctor wants to see you before he goes, sir," he said.

The pathologist was standing on the makeshift inspection platform, his perennially silent assistant, Burns, at his side.

Detective Inspector Sloan and Detective Constable Crosby clambered up beside them. There was room—but only just—for the four of them. Dyson and Williams had finished their photography and were standing at the bottom of the scaffolding tower. Also waiting at ground level at a discreet distance was a van from Morton's, the Berebury undertakers.

"Eyes first, hands next, tongue last, Sloan," said Dr. Dabbe. "That's what I was taught."

"Very wise, Doctor," said Sloan. At the Police Training College they had had a lot to say about ears and listening but there was no need to go into that now.

"Poor Fred who was alive and is dead." Detective Constable Crosby had not been taught anything of the kind and rushed into speech.

"Very dead," agreed the pathologist before Sloan could say anything at all. "Well, gentlemen, we've done all that we can up here." He looked round from their raised vantage-point. "I must say it makes a change from a ditch."

"Yes, Doctor," said Sloan. Now the doctor came to mention it, most dead bodies were low-lying.

"The heights of Abraham's bosom," said Dr Dabbe obscurely.

Sloan cleared his throat. "What do you make of him, Doctor? For the report, I mean."

"Oh, there's not a lot of doubt about the NASH classification, Sloan," said the pathologist, "unless someone removed the head for fun, of course."

"What's the NASH classification?" enquired Crosby.

"The four options open to a forensic pathologist," responded Dr. Dabbe, waving a hand in the direction of the skeleton.

"Four?" echoed the constable.

"Four, Crosby," snapped Sloan. The constable should know all this. "One more than three, and one less than five." He wasn't sure if it was a good thing that the pathologist encouraged badinage with constables. Superintendent Leeyes didn't.

"Natural causes, accident, suicide and homicide," recited Dr. Dabbe.

"NASH," agreed Crosby, nodding.

"Homicide, Crosby," said Sloan mordantly. "The killing of a man. Like regicide but less specific."

"Of course," said the pathologist, momentarily diverted, "there are always the other four things."

"What other four, Doctor?" enquired Sloan evenly. They

weren't getting anywhere standing upon the platform talking like this, and time might be important.

"Eschatology."

"What's that?" asked Crosby promptly. It sounded like a medical word to Sloan.

"The science of the four last things," said Dr. Dabbe.

Sloan didn't say anything at all. The doctor was going to tell them whether or not he asked what they were.

"Death, judgement, heaven and hell," pronounced Dr. Dabbe. He grinned suddenly and tapped the scaffolding platform with his foot. "Makes you feel you're in a pulpit, doesn't it, being up here?"

The height wasn't having that effect on Sloan, besides which he had other things on his mind. "The finger," he began purposefully. In his opinion philosophy could wait. There were certain practical matters he needed to set in train. And soon. "Can we be sure that it came from this body?"

"As sure as eggs is eggs," responded the pathologist just a whit colloquially, "but I'll check for you properly presently."

"Thank you."

"Actually, Sloan, nearly all the fingers have gone, give or take a thumb."

"'The moving finger—'" began Crosby.

Sloan quelled the detective constable with a look. The trouble was that he couldn't do that with the consultant pathologist to the Berebury District General Hospital Management Group.

"So," continued Dr. Dabbe obliviously, "have quite a number of other smaller bones." He coughed. "And we shan't be wanting a lot in the way of Canopic jars, shall we, Burns?"

"No, Doctor."

Sloan waited for elucidation.

"They're what the ancient Egyptians used to bury the entrails in," the doctor informed him.

"When they weren't casting them?" enquired Sloan neatly.

"That was the Greeks," said Dr. Dabbe.

"Talking of height"—Sloan reverted to an earlier topic before he got into deeper water still—"do we know how tall this man was?"

"Burns here has done some measurements," said Dr. Dabbe. "Haven't you, Burns?"

"That's right, Doctor."

"And taking the length of the left femur—"

"That's still there, then," said Sloan.

"Too heavy for anything short of a vulture," said th
pathologist. "Or a jackal."

"So . . ." The only jackals in rural Calleshire were huma
ones.

"So, taking the known length of the left femur, measured
of course, from the top of its head to the bottom of th
internal condylar surface—"

"Of course," murmured Sloan.

"—and applying Pearson's formula for the reconstruction c
living stature from dead long bones—"

"Yes?"

"—we can calculate that he—whoever he was—"

Who he was, thought Sloan to himself, was a bigge
question altogether. Perhaps who he had been might be
better way of putting it. He permitted himself a sideway
glance at what was lying there. A quotation drifted into hi
mind from somewhere. "A rag and a bone and a hank o
hair," except that there wasn't a rag left on the body and n
hair either.

"—whoever he was," repeated Dr. Dabbe, "was just ove
five foot eight inches tall."

"That's very useful to know," said Sloan and he meant it

"Give or take half an inch or so," the pathologist said
adding a rider.

"A small man, then."

"By the time I tell the court in centimetres," said th
pathologist cynically, "they won't know whether he was
dwarf or a giant."

Sloan nodded in sympathy. Metrication was yet anothe
hazard to clear thought by members of juries. "And are there
any—er—pointers at all to the cause of death, Doctor?" He
had an ingrained objection to using the word "clue."

"None that I could see from where I had to stand,"
admitted the pathologist cheerfully. "I might be able to be
more helpful, though, after we've got him down off the slope
of Mount Parnassus here and back in the mortuary."

"Quite so," said Sloan. He agreed that these were not idea
for proper scientific examination.

"Although," said Dr. Dabbe, "how that's going to be done
I really don't know."

"Dead man's lift?" suggested Crosby brightly.

"You had better go down first, Crosby," said Sloan repressively.

Dr. Dabbe was still considering the skeleton. "There's one thing I can't tell you yet, Sloan."

"What's that, Doctor?"

"At exactly what stage the head came off."

Sloan cleared his throat. "It would be a help to know."

"It didn't fall off, Sloan, that's for sure."

"No, Doctor." Sloan hadn't supposed that for one moment that it had.

"But," said the pathologist, "I can tell you how it came off."

That, too, thought Sloan, would be useful information. The police didn't have a lot in the way of hard facts yet. Crosby had started to swing off the platform and onto the top of the ladder as Dr. Dabbe spoke. He paused.

"Someone used an instrument," said Dr. Dabbe.

"What sort of instrument?" asked Sloan cautiously.

"A cleaver of some kind. An axe, perhaps, or a butcher's knife." There was a sudden change in atmosphere on the makeshift scaffolding tower. The banter had gone. Now the pathologist was deadly serious. "And I should say—mind you, Sloan, I'm speaking without a microscope—"

"Yes, Doctor?" Out of the corner of his eye Sloan could see Crosby poised at the top of the ladder listening too.

"—that the head came off in one fell blow," said the doctor chillingly.

Sloan absorbed the information without comment. Even some professional executioners hadn't managed that. Something gruesome about the beheading of one of the wives of Henry the Eighth came into his mind. Or had it been Mary, Queen of Scots?

"An axe, you said, Doctor," murmured Sloan. The police needed to know what to look for. And where to start looking. Firemen had axes, didn't they? Even part-time firemen.

"I can't tell you exactly what was used." Dr. Dabbe frowned. "Something heavy and sharp."

"It was a clean cut, anyway," said Sloan. Somehow "clean" didn't seem quite the right adjective but he couldn't call another, better one to mind just at this moment.

The pathologist nodded. "Between Atlas and axis, if you really want to know."

It would come up as something quite different in Dr. Dabbe's report to the coroner, Sloan knew that.

Dr. Dabbe grinned. "The first cervical vertebra and epistropheus, actually."

"Does that presuppose any sort of knowledge on the part of who did it, Doctor?"

The medical man considered this. "I daresay most farmers pick up a working knowledge of anatomy over the years, Sloan. And, of course, there used to be a fair bit of pole axeing in the old days." He prepared to follow Crosby down the ladder. "My guess is that when you find the head you'll find the cause of death—unless it was a straightforward decapitation, that is."

"Yes, Doctor." Instituting a search for a severed head was something else to be done with all possible speed. And this time they couldn't exclude wooded land. A human agency had been involved. Unlike crows, human beings weren't afraid of predators.

The pathologist took one last look at the bones on the barn roof. "A good thing that those crows had been properly brought up, Sloan, isn't it?"

"Beg pardon, Doctor?"

"They left something for Mr. Manners, like Nanny always said."

"But not a lot," said Crosby, disappearing down the ladder.

TWELVE

•

O let no evil dreams be near

"Mrs. Mellot didn't say a word," said Detective Constable
Crosby to Sloan as they walked back across the farmyard
towards the house and parlour. "Not a word. Not all the while
I was there, anyway." He sniffed. "Mum's the word with her
all right."

"Actions speak louder than words," said Sloan firmly. There
had been no disguising the swift rush of blood from Meg
Mellot's face when naked fear had struck. As Sloan stepped
over the farm threshold now something came back to him over
the years from an English lesson—something that that arch-
observer William Shakespeare had noted. It had been in one
of those plays that for some reason teachers of English literature lingered over—he of the two parts, *King Henry the Fourth*.

> "The whiteness of thy cheek
> Is apter than thy tongue to tell thy errand."

He remembered the fight scenes, too. They were really
what made it a good play for boys—and the part of Sir John
Falstaff inevitably going to the fattest boy in the class...

"She didn't speak, you said," murmured Sloan to Crosby.
Something else that came welling out of his subconscious was
the wartime slogan "Be like Dad, keep Mum."

"There wasn't a dicky-bird out of her," said Detective
Constable Crosby, who had not been thinking about either
Shakespeare's plays or propaganda posters. "The dog would
have barked, sir, for sure, though, if anyone else had humped
that body up on the roof. That was what it was there for—to
bark."

"A watch-dog," said Sloan precisely. He'd seen a hole in a
wall for a watch-dog once and the phrase had fallen into place
in his mind. It had been in the ruins of an abbey which he
and his wife, Margaret, had visited one holiday. There had
been an elliptical gap at the height of a dog exactly opposite

109

the abbey gate and the dog was expected to bark when anyone came near. They had had a death's door there, too. For a moment Sloan had thought that the abbey custodian had been joking.

He wasn't. He'd led their party to the wall of the north chancel and pointed. "There you are," he'd said for all to hear. "Death's door."

It was the custodian's party piece and he had done it well. It was, he had explained, a door in the abbey wall which led directly to the abbey cemetery. It was only opened on the death of a monk to let the body and its cortége through for burial. All that Sloan had been able to think about at the time had been the hoary—and very irreverent—medical chestnut about the patient "being at death's door but the doctor hoped to pull him through." The sight had stuck in his memory all the same.

There was another phrase though—a more modern one— that was rather more germane to the present. It came straight from Sir Arthur Conan Doyle.

"'The curious incident of the dog in the night-time,'" quoted Sloan from *Silver Blaze*.

"That's right, sir." Crosby scratched his brow. "Why didn't the Mellots just say they'd heard Fido barking? That's all they needed to do, isn't it?"

"It may not have been true," said Sloan mildly. There was something in the Bible about that. He quoted it. "What is truth? saith Pilate."

Crosby looked distinctly doubtful.

"Moreover," pointed out Sloan, "the body may not have been put up on the roof at night."

"But—"

"We don't know for certain that it was." Sloan tightened his lips. Actually they knew very little for certain at the moment and that was a worry in itself.

Crosby looked even more doubtful. "If it went up there—"

"Was put." Sloan corrected him at once. Life was quite complicated enough without bringing levitation into the picture—even for "the friendless bodies of unburied men."

"Was put up there in daylight," said Crosby, "and the Mellots didn't know, then that means that Len Hodge did— does—know. Bound to."

"He might have been got out of the way," said Sloan, leading the way down the passage.

"He knows something, sir," insisted Crosby. "Ted Mason says so."

Sloan nodded. An interview with Len Hodge had a high priority. But so did further words with George and Meg Mellot. He pushed open the garden door and said, "Feeling better now, are you, madam?"

Meg Mellot nodded, her face still a chalky white. She was sitting bolt upright on the couch now but she still did not look well.

Sloan began the interview without preamble. "I've been finding out a little more about Mellot's Furnishings."

"Upholsterers to the Nation," responded Crosby upon the instant, demonstrating that he was as susceptible as the next man to a good advertising slogan.

"Ivor Harbeton's company," went on Sloan, gritting his teeth and rising above the television demotic, "made a bid for Mellot's Furnishings at the end of April this year."

"Conway's Covers," said George Mellot wearily. "That was the company that Harbeton used for the attack." The farmer was sitting on the sofa beside his wife looking years older than he had done the day before.

Sloan continued his narrative. "Mellot's Furnishings turned down their approaches flat." It was company mergers that could be compared with marriages, wasn't it?

George Mellot stirred himself. "Absolutely flat," he agreed. "Tom wouldn't hear of it. The firm was his baby and he wanted to keep it that way."

"So Conway's Covers tried again," said Sloan. Take-overs had more in common with shotgun weddings than with arranged marriages.

Mellot moistened his lips. "That was at the beginning of May."

"With a higher bid," added Sloan. A marriage of convenience, perhaps.

"If at first you don't succeed," interposed Crosby sententiously, "try, try again."

Detective Inspector Sloan bit back the first response that came into his head and said instead, "That's just what Harbeton did." Marriage à la mode, that was it.

"He kept on coming back," said George Mellot dully.

His wife said nothing.

Crosby looked quite interested for once. "And what did Mellot's Furnishings do?"

"Fought it tooth and nail," said Sloan succinctly. The man in the City had promised to let him have copies of the series of letters to shareholders and the newspaper advertising campaign that had constituted the ammunition of war. Bid followed by counterbid. Salvo by countersalvo. Or had it really been dowry all the time? Pretty reading, the City man had said they made. Pleas for support from shareholders from the embattled Board of Directors of Mellot's Furnishings; bait laid in front of those same shareholders by the predatory Conway's Covers board, chaired by Ivor Harbeton; appeals to sentiment; appeals to greed. He turned to George Mellot. "I'm not boring you, sir, I trust."

"No, Inspector," replied the farmer with all the searing astringency of rhatany root, "you're not boring me. I'm listening."

"Who won?" enquired Detective Constable Crosby as if the saga had the simplicity of a bedtime story.

Detective Inspector Sloan switched his gaze from one man to the other and regarded his subordinate with a certain academic interest. Not for Crosby the majestic cadences of the Edwardian versifier whose sentiments seemed to be the hallmark of every speech on every Speech Day. "He marks—not that you won or lost—but how you played the game."

Perhaps it was as well. Take-over battles did not sound particularly sporting—or sportive—affairs.

"The goodies or the baddies?" asked Crosby before he could speak.

That simplified the situation still further. Crosby's interest though was better than the monumental indifference of the sheep in the next field at the Battle of Hastings that Sloan's history teacher had brought to the attention of the class. He had been pointing a different moral, of course. "Always remember," the schoolmaster had been fond of saying, "that while one of the most decisive battles in English history was being fought out the sheep in the next field went on eating. Before, during and after the battle." And a young Christopher Dennis Sloan had dutifully remembered, though for the life of him—then or now—he wasn't sure what to think about it.

Detective Inspector Sloan, working policeman on duty, couldn't let a little philosophy come between him and the business at hand. He said courteously, "Perhaps Mr. Mellot would like to tell us who won."

The farmer said, "It isn't as straightforward as that, Inspector."

"No?" said Sloan pleasantly. "No, perhaps not. Your brother Tom gave Ivor Harbeton a run for his money, though,
didn't he?" There, for a wonder, was a cliché that filled the
bill.

"He did," responded Mellot with spirit. Meg Mellot still
stayed silent and withdrawn.

"Bully for him," said Crosby laconically.

Sloan resumed his role as narrator. It seemed easier. "So
Ivor Harbeton tried something different."

"Robert the Bruce's spider," remarked Crosby unnecessarily, "just went on."

"A dawn raid," said George Mellot dully. "That was what
came next."

Detective Constable Crosby brightened immediately. They
had dawn raids in the police force: exciting, truly clandestine
affairs, when hardened criminals were tumbled out of bed in
the middle of the night. He said so.

"Not that sort of dawn raid," said Detective Inspector
Sloan, very nearly at the end of his patience with his subordinate. The man in the Fraud Squad had just explained to him
the City's version of the tactic. It was rather different from
the police one.

It wasn't very long before he found himself explaining it to
Superintendent Leeyes too.

"The buyer, sir," Sloan informed him presently down the
telephone, "starts the whole thing by building up various
small holdings in the company that they want to buy."

Like Mr. Dick, Superintendent Leeyes was more interested in a head. "It must be somewhere, Sloan," he insisted.
Some there be that have no Memorial but not King Charles
the First.

"Yes, sir," agreed Sloan at once. "Naturally."

His superior officer's voice came testily down the telephone line. "I hope you're looking for it then."

"I am in the process of making arrangements to do so, sir."
It would be the superintendent's King Charles's head if they
weren't careful.

"That means you haven't started yet," pounced Leeyes,
who had not risen to the rank of superintendent by the
exercising of the gentler virtues.

"Not exactly started," agreed Sloan. "Not yet. But it is at
hand." He tried not to sound too defensive. "It's a matter of

arranging for a special photographic survey of the area." Sloan
did not pretend to understand the technicalities of infra-red
cameras but there were modern—ultramodern—methods available now for spotting patches of land where earth had been
disturbed.

Leeyes grunted. "When I was a constable we looked the
hard way with water-jugs."

"Sir?"

"You're too young to remember," said Leeyes loftily. "A
straight line of men pouring water on the ground out of jugs
as they walked forward, that's how it used to be done."

"But—"

"If the ground hadn't been touched," Leeyes informed
him, "the water ran straight off."

"I see, sir."

"If it had been turned over to bury something," swept on
Leeyes, "the water soaked straight in. You're a gardener,
Sloan. You should know that."

"Yes, sir."

"Cheaper, too."

"We haven't defined the area that needs searching, sir, yet.
Not for the head."

Leeyes grunted unhelpfully. "I must say a farm's a fine
place anyway to be looking for ground that's just been turned.
They're always having a go at it on a farm."

"There's the wood, too, sir," Sloan reminded him. "There's
something in the wood and the cameras aren't going to help
there." The wood was one of his worries. He shot out his
wrist and looked at his watch. It was too soon for more news
from Dr. Dabbe. "What we need is daylight and there won't
be enough of that now until tomorrow." Some things, though,
could go ahead. He'd sent Crosby up to Stanestede Farm and
put out a general alert for Tom Mellot. He could explain
about Ivor Harbeton to the superintendent, too, if only he
would let him.

He tried again.

"As I said, sir," he began smoothly, "the buyer starts the
whole thing by building up various small holdings in the
company that they want to buy."

"Mellot's Furnishings," grunted Leeyes. "Go on."

"They were cast in the role of victim," agreed Sloan.

"And the raptor was Ivor Harbeton's company, I suppose,"
said Leeyes.

"Beg pardon, sir?"

"Raptors are birds of prey, Sloan." One memorable winter the superintendent had attended a series of evening classes on ornithology. This had had two unfortunate results. He became known among the younger constables as the Birdman of Berebury, which was bad for discipline, and he fell out with the Town Council, which had a bylaw prohibiting the feeding of pigeons in public places. This was bad for everyone.

"The company doing the buying," Sloan forged on, "hopes that nobody will notice what they are up to."

"Ha!"

"Sometimes," continued Sloan doggedly, "they even sell some of their holdings, too, to stop anyone becoming suspicious."

"Makes larceny seem quite simple, Sloan, doesn't it?"

"Some stockbrokers won't do it," pointed out Sloan fairly.

"And some, I suppose," remarked Leeyes genially, "specialise in it."

"It is a white-collar crime," agreed Sloan tacitly.

"Fraud usually is," commented Leeyes at his sagest, "unless you count the three-card trick."

Sloan kept steadfastly to the business at hand. "Of course, they don't do the buying in their own names."

"Aliases?" said Leeyes alertly. "Do they use aliases?"

"They call them nominees," said Sloan delicately.

"I call them men of straw," remarked Leeyes.

"But," Sloan quoted his mentor in the City of London, "undisclosed holdings above a certain limit are not allowed."

"Sloan," came the swift answer down the line, "I may have retained my youth but I have been a policeman long enough to know the difference between 'not allowed' and 'not done.'"

"Yes, sir."

"So . . ."

"So there comes a moment when the buyer has to make that disclosure."

"A law, is it, Sloan?"

"A code, sir," he said. Even lesser breeds without the law had codes of conduct. Sometimes, of course, codes worked better than laws. Sometimes they didn't.

"So that's how this character Ivor Harbeton started to get his claws into Mellot's Furnishings, is it?"

"In a manner of speaking, sir." Now he came to think about it, perhaps "raptor" was the right word. "He got his hands on just under thirty percent of the equity," said Sloan, consulting his notebook.

Leeyes grunted.

"That's near enough," explained Sloan, "to the crucial figure for going into the market early one morning for the final killing which would have given Ivor Harbeton control." When a bird of prey made its descent out of the sky down onto its victim it was called a stoop: even Sloan knew that.

There was a short silence while Superintendent Leeyes digested this information. "That's when he disappeared, I suppose."

"It is," said Sloan. "And that's not all, sir."

"No?"

"In the beginning Mellot's Furnishings wasn't wholly owned by Tom Mellot and his wife," said Sloan. "The man in the City had them look it up for me."

"Well?"

"George Mellot and his wife put up half the original capital."

Leeyes grunted.

Sloan pulled his notebook towards him. "I think we may find, sir, that Tom Mellot has a half share in Pencombe Farm."

"And I think," said Superintendent Leeyes weightily, "that the sooner someone has a little chat with Mr. Tom Mellot the better."

THIRTEEN

•

Stand in awe and sin not

"Just one or two questions, madam, if you don't mind." Detective Constable Crosby slipped smoothly into his professional patter as soon as the door of Stanestede Farm was opened to him. "May I come in?"

Mrs. Andrina Ritchie was obviously less used to the interview routine and visibly braced herself. "Of course . . ."

"It would help a lot if we could trace your husband." He coughed. "In the circumstances, if you take my meaning."

She nodded. "I have heard about—about Pencombe."

"The easiest way to trace a man," said Crosby, "is usually through his car."

"His car's here," she said slowly. "In the garage."

"But—"

"It was found at Calleford Market the next day. The day after he'd gone, I mean." She gave him a brittle look. "The auctioneers rang up and said they'd noticed it was still at the market and was there anything wrong."

"So you went in and collected it."

"George Mellot very kindly ran me over to Calleford."

"The keys?"

"Under the mat of the driver's seat where we always left them."

Crosby shook his head sorrowfully at the monumental folly of this practice. "Were you surprised about the car still being there?"

"Less surprised than I would have been," she admitted frankly, "if our solicitor hadn't telephoned me before the auctioneers did."

"Oh?"

"It was old Mr. Puckle from Puckle, Puckle and Nunnery. He told me he had had a telephone call from Martin that morning."

"The Friday?"

"That's right. Mr. Puckle had been in court but Martin had left a message with his secretary to say he was walking away

117

from his old life completely and would Mr. Puckle see to everything."

Crosby wrote that down.

"More like walking away from his old wife," she said bitterly.

Crosby said nothing

"You can't just slough off the past like a snake shedding its skin," she said with anguish. "Can you?"

"No, madam." A lot of people, though, thought that you could—until, that is, they tried it and found that you couldn't. Crosby knew that. Like Christian in *The Pilgrim's Progress* you took your scars with you. And kept them until the end of life.

"Mr. Puckle said to carry on as usual for the time being." She snorted gently. "As usual!"

"Yes, madam." Solicitors didn't like action. Crosby knew that, too. The only matter that stirred them into speedy action that Crosby knew about was the making of a will. They came round pretty quickly if you wanted to write a new will. "So . . ."

"So that's what I've been doing." She twisted her hands together. "It hasn't been easy, I can tell you."

"No, madam." The constable cleared his throat preparatory to speech. There was one question that was always more delicate than the rest. "What are you doing about money?" he asked.

"We had a joint account," she answered tonelessly.

Sauce for the goose and sauce for the gander, was what Crosby called those. "And has it been used by your husband?" he asked curiously.

She shook her head. "Not since the beginning of June. That's the funny thing. I asked the bank especially." Her lips tightened. "I thought he would have emptied it, you see. It would have been just like him."

"But he hadn't?"

"He hasn't touched a penny," she said.

Mate and checkmate.

"Perhaps Beverley whoever she is can afford to keep him in the style to which he would like to be accustomed," she said.

Or cheque-mate.

"But the farm—" began Crosby aloud.

"That's a proper partnership," she said. "It's in both our names. All signed and sealed and everything."

So was marriage, but Crosby didn't say so.

"We were in Stanestede together," she said, "as joint owners, each with power to act. That was in case anything happened. That's why Mr. Puckle told me to do nothing and to carry on on my own. He said Martin might come back and then..." Her voice trailed away disconsolately.

"It would help us if he did," said the constable truthfully. Crosby wasn't sure how Andrina Ritchie would feel about this in the long run but the police would be very glad indeed if he did. His mind was on a skeleton at Pencombe and narrowing the field always helped. "There's just one more thing, madam."

"Yes?" she said. Detective Constable Crosby noticed the almost subconscious squaring of Andrina Ritchie's shoulders as she spoke to him.

"How tall is your husband?" The shoulders slackened. It wasn't the question she had been expecting, he was sure about that.

She frowned. "Isn't it silly?" she said. "I'm not sure. He was about five foot eight or nine, I suppose."

Crosby wrote that down. "I expect he took his passport with him." A new life might well begin in another country; it wouldn't be the first time that had happened.

"Passport!" she echoed with contumely. "Martin hadn't got a passport. You don't travel if you're tied to a farm."

"No, I suppose you don't." Crosby could see this. A passport, though, would have Martin Ritchie's exact height on it and Dr. Dabbe would tell them the height of the dead man. And if two and two made four...

"A farm is a millstone round your neck," she said.

"I can see that it might be."

"All the time."

"Yes, madam." Crosby knew the formula for calculating height from a thigh-bone now. He wondered if there was one for doing the same thing from a pair of trousers. Or if you used the same formula. Cuff to ankle might give you height too, if you had the ankle, that is....

"You can't escape from a farm," said Andrina Ritchie.

"Could I see some of his clothes, please?" There was a code that men's outfitters used for selling off-the-peg suits that might help too. The only letters of it that Crosby knew, though, were S.P. and they stood for short and portly. He didn't know any short and portly farmers.

She led the way to a bedroom furnished almost entirely in

white and opened the doors of a wardrobe that extended all the way along one wall. "Martin's things are at this end."

Detective Constable Crosby picked out a dark suit.

"His best," she said promptly. "His 'Sunday-go-meeting' suit, he called it." Her lips twisted. "His 'Thursday-go-meeting-Beverley' suit was more free and easy."

Martin Ritchie wasn't short and portly. Crosby could tell that at once. If his suit was anything to go by he was a well-built medium man. "A photograph might help us trace him," said Crosby.

Andrina Ritchie moved to a drawer and pulled out an album. "Take your pick," she said savagely. "I shan't be wanting them any more."

Crosby tucked the album under his arm. "What colour is his hair?"

"Light ginger," said Andrina Ritchie, "and if it's any help he had freckles."

"It is a help," responded Crosby gravely.

"More in summer than in winter, of course."

"Naturally, madam." He fingered his notebook. "Is there anything else that would help us to build up a picture of him?"

"He didn't have any distinguishing marks, if that's what you mean." She examined her own manicured fingernails with studied interest.

Crosby kept silent. The heap of bones that had been on the barn roof had gone a long way past distinguishing marks.

"Except an appendix scar," she volunteered. "He had that."

"Nothing—er—deeper?" Crosby hunted about in his mind for a more graphic way of putting what he wanted to say and couldn't find it.

Mrs. Ritchie frowned. "I think he broke a rib once. There was some trouble once with a bull."

Crosby didn't know if that would still show or not. Dr. Dabbe would find it if it did. Another thought came to him. Diamonds were forever but gold lasted well too. "His teeth," he said.

"What about them?" asked Andrina Ritchie, raising a pair of finely plucked eyebrows into an arch.

"Were they all there, for instance?"

"He had a crown on one front one that he'd had knocked out."

"Another bull?"

"A hockey match," she said distastefully.

"Ah."

"A mixed hockey match," she added with dryness.

"Heroes' hockey," pronounced Crosby. "That's what that's called."

"And he had a bit of a gap on one side at the back. That's all."

"It may be enough," said Crosby, shutting his notebook and picking up Martin Ritchie's best suit. "You never know, do you, madam?"

The detective who went round to call on Tom Mellot's family home in a rather nice cul-de-sac in a pleasant part of London was something of a linguist. He was also both young and personable He had in fact been hand-picked for the job: Detective Inspector Sloan had asked the Metropolitan Police to send the best Spanish-speaking range-finder they had. Kitchen range-finder, that is. He had gone to the Mellots' in response to an urgent message from the Calleshire County Constabulary.

"Buenos días, señorita." He had begun on exactly the right note with the au pair girl who had answered the door and within minutes he was established where he wanted to be—on a chair drawn up to the kitchen table, a dish of tapas in front of him.

Teresita Losada pulled up the chair opposite to his and expanded in Spanish in a way that would have astonished her employers, who had found her uncommunicative and inclined to fall into peninsular—if not positively oriental—reveries. Warnings about talking to strangers uttered by Mrs. Tom Mellot did not extend in Teresita's mind to handsome young man familiar with the argot of Cartagena. Even the mandatory mention of the dreaded word "police" by the young man did not upset her. In her way of thinking there was absolutely no connection between this agreeable listener and the Guardia Civil, still less with the Policía Armada y de Tráfico. Besides, were not the British police wonderful? Everyone said so.

"Muchas gracias," said the detective with the good manners to the offer of the bowl of tapas. Teresita Losada was too young and innocent to have encountered the Cuerpo General

de Policía—the plain-clothes Criminal Investigation Branch of
the Spanish Police. The detective quickly found out, as
George Mellot had done before him, that the au pair did not
know where Tom Mellot and his wife and family were.

"They are away," said Teresita vaguely. "They will come
back."

"Naturally," said the young detective in his best Spanish.
"I understand. *'Le weekend.'*" Too late he remembered that
this was predominantly a French expression but the girl did
not seem to have noticed. He steered the conversation gently
away from the difficulties of getting really good olive oil in
this part of London—first pressing, naturally—and instead
talked about the firm of Mellot's Furnishings Ltd. and what
had happened to them last May.

"*Esa empresa!*" exclaimed Teresita dramatically, throwing
up her hands.

"Tell me," said the detective.

"What a time we had," she said impressively. "You would
not believe it."

"No?"

"Always the telephone. Morning, noon and night, it rings."

"Ah . . ."

"And men always talking, talking, talking."

The man from the police made sympathetic noises but did
not say much.

"And me," she said, "me, I have to look after the children
all of that time because everyone is so busy." She pouted. "To
keep them from being under the feet."

"You must have been very busy," said the other diplomatically.
"What was all the fuss about? Did you know?"

"Business," said Teresita dismissively. Women's lib was not
as far along the road in Spain as it was in Great Britain. It had
got nowhere at all in Teresita's village. "Men's work." She
nodded in a way that would have disappointed not a few
feminists.

The personable young detective nodded encouragingly.

"Mrs. Mellot she did try to explain it to me one day." The
girl got up from the table to give a stir to a dish of paella on
the stove.

"Ah . . ."

"But I did not understand," she said. The great thing about
the British way of life that Teresita Losada had grasped was

that duennas had no place in it. Nothing else was really important to her.

"I see." The accommodating young man contrived to sound sympathetic.

She frowned. "I think it was that someone wanted to take their enterprise from them and they did not want that." In Spain, too, having and holding went together.

"Naturally, señorita," said the young man fluently, "no one enjoys losing what is theirs." Every policeman found that out very early on in his career. He slid a photograph of Ivor Harbeton onto the table. It was a press photograph and not a very good one at that—he was certainly no hidalgo—but Ivor Harbeton had been divorced not once but three times and there was no one on hand to supply a better one. His last known address was an expensive service flat. Nothing remained there to show who its last occupant had been. "Tell me, did this man ever come to this house?"

Teresita Losada peered at the picture and nodded. "Yes, he came here. I saw him."

"Many times?"

She shook her head. "Once only." She set a plate of paella in front of the policeman.

"When? Can you remember?"

She searched for the right words. "Just before the end of the busy time."

"Did you have to take the children out when he came?" he asked indistinctly between mouthfuls of paella.

Her brow puckered. "The children were in bed."

"He came late at night then?"

She looked blank. "Not particularly."

The detective metaphorically kicked himself. He should have remembered that to a nation that starts its evening meal after ten o'clock no such time as "late at night" exists.

"I remember," said Teresita, "because I had to take the dog out."

"I see." The paella was good.

"I do not like taking the dog out."

"No?"

"The dog does not like me." This was Teresita's only failing in an alien land. The judgement of a small white Sealyham terrier was not wrong either. Her employers had found her kind to children but not to animals.

The detective got back to the matter at hand. He tapped

the photograph of Harbeton. "How long did this man stay here?"

She shrugged her shoulders. "Who can say?"

"What do you mean?"

"I did not see him leave."

"He had gone by the time you got back to the house?"

She opened her hands wide. "I do not know. Mrs. Mellot told me when I came in that it was time for bed."

"His car?" said the detective immediately. "Was that still standing outside when you came back with the dog?"

"There was no car," she said. "He came by taxi nearly."

"Nearly?" For a moment the young man thought he had lost an idiom somewhere.

"I saw him come," she said simply. "He got out of the taxi at the end of the road and walked the rest of the way. He came nearly."

The detective nodded, satisfied. Ivor Harbeton had come to see Tom Mellot for a secret meeting then, between principals, advisers out of the way, tell-tale company cars left in the garage. Business battles usually came down to this in the end—an eyeball-to-eyeball with seconds out of the ring. It wasn't so far removed from a medieval tournament and knights jousting after all.

He finished his paella before he brought the conversation round to Ivor Harbeton again: and he did that casually. "You don't remember which day of the week it was, do you?"

She didn't but he didn't mind. In fact he executed a little passacaglia all by himself as he went down the garden path and said "*Olé*" under his breath when he finished his report.

"Tomorrow," Teresita Losada had said hopefully, "I make fabada."

Detective Inspector Sloan regarded the suit which Crosby had brought back from Stanestede Farm for a long moment and then said confidently, "Ernest Grimshaw will know." He looked up. "What time is it, Crosby?"

"Half past eight, sir."

"Couldn't be better," said Sloan briskly. "He'll be back from chapel by now. The car, Crosby. You can take me there straightaway."

"Take you where, sir?"

"Postlethwaite and Grimshaw's in the High Street."

"That crummy outfit?"

"Outfitters, Crosby," Sloan corrected him gently. "Gents' outfitters, to be precise."

"They're still crummy."

"Old-fashioned," said Sloan. But that was an understatement and Sloan knew it. The firm of Postlethwaite and Grimshaw was among the oldest in Berebury and very proud of the fact. The last Postlethwaite had died in the Old Queen's time—they had put up black mourning-boards over the shop-windows on the day of the funeral naturally—but there were still Grimshaws in the business.

"They won't be open on a Sunday evening," objected Crosby.

"Ernest Grimshaw," said Sloan impressively, "is probably the only man who actually still lives in the High Street."

"Over the shop?" said Crosby.

"His grandfather slept under the counter," said Sloan. "Come on, Crosby, and bring that suit with you."

What he did not tell Crosby was that he knew the shop well. It was in Postlethwaite and Grimshaw's shop that he, Christopher Dennis Sloan, had had his first pair of long trousers bought for him. In Sloan's childhood "going into longs" had almost had the quality of a rite of passage. As the police car swept down the Sabbath-deserted High Street he wondered what symbolic rite among growing boys had succeeded it to make the transition stage between boyhood and youth manifest to the world.

Mr. Ernest Grimshaw's first reaction on seeing Martin Ritchie's suit was to feel the material between his fingers. "Nothing wrong with this cloth, Inspector. Run-of-the-mill, of course, but nearly everything is these days, more's the pity."

"It's not the cloth that we've come about, Mr. Grimshaw." Detective Inspector Sloan and Detective Constable Crosby had interrupted a Sunday-evening-after-chapel cold supper of veal and ham pie that was in its way as ritual as any feast in the church's calendar.

"Mass-produced, of course," said the shopkeeper, turning the jacket over in his hands. "There's not a lot of bespoke tailoring about any more." Old Mr. Grimshaw's energies were engaged in fighting a rearguard action against the multiple retail stores. Postlethwaite and Grimshaw's premises occupied a prime site in the High Street and Ernest Grimshaw knew it. Young Mr. Grimshaw's attentions centred largely on trying to bring the firm into the second half of the twentieth

century. He was doomed to failure in this: his father had been
the last man in Berebury to stop wearing spats. "Or good
cloth, either," continued Ernest Grimshaw, who continually
lamented the passing of palmier days. "You don't see as much
worsted about as you used to, more's the pity."

"Things aren't what they were," said Sloan generally. He
had found that this remark usually evoked ready sympathy
with anyone on the graveyard side of sixty. It should go down
well with the owner of the last emporium in the town to have
had an overhead cash railway. Sloan could still remember the
fascination with which he had watched the little brass cylin-
der with his mother's money in it travel to the lady cashier in
her perch in the middle of the shop and back with the receipt
and the change. The policeman in him now knew how
vulnerable the cashier had been. The little boy in him still
saw the mechanism as something that the wonders of the
space age had not diminished.

"Near the top of the range, of course," said Mr. Grimshaw,
looking over the whole of Martin Ritchie's outfit with a
professional eye, "but not quite at the top."

"What we wanted to know," said Sloan, "was whether you
could tell us how tall the man who wore it was."

Mr. Grimshaw dropped the suit back onto the table rather
quickly.

"A little matter," explained Sloan, "of our having the suit on
the one hand and some human remains on the other."

"Quite, quite," said Mr. Grimshaw hurriedly. "I thought
there would be—ah—a reason. It being—ah—Sunday evening and so forth. How tall, did you say?"

"I wouldn't have been seen dead in it myself," remarked
Crosby chattily.

Mr. Grimshaw had already taken a quick look at what the
detective constable was wearing and averted his eyes.

"How tall," concurred Sloan pacifically.

"Let me have a look at the trousers then." Mr. Grimshaw
felt about round his own lapels for the tape measure which
lived over his shoulders from Monday morning to Saturday
evening. When his hands came back empty he looked at
them in some surprise. "Where did I put my inch tape?" he
murmured.

"The inside trouser leg measures thirty inches," supplied
Crosby.

"Then the wearer will have been between five foot eight

and five foot nine tall," pronounced Mr. Grimshaw promptly. He looked up. "Is that what you wanted to know, Inspector?"

"It is a fact," temporised Sloan, "and facts are always helpful in our work, Mr. Grimshaw." Who was it who had said that there were no problems, only missing data? At least Martin Ritchie's height was a little less missing data.

"That's off the cuff, of course, Inspector," said the outfitter.

"Naturally," said Sloan. It was every man to his own metaphor. He picked up the trousers.

"They would fit our body," remarked Crosby less discreetly.

Mention of the word "body" aroused Mr. Grimshaw's professional memory. "We used to do a steady trade in white silk stockings for laying out," he said, shaking his head sadly, "but there's no call for them any more."

"You wouldn't be seen dead in them either, Crosby, I suppose," said Sloan sourly. He thanked Mr. Grimshaw and reached for Martin Ritchie's coat and trousers. "Come on. We've still got work to do."

FOURTEEN

•

The grave to be a bed of hope

The primitive instinct to congregate can be observed in almost all animal species, not least the human variety. Sociologists have noted that this herd instinct is powerfully reinforced by exciting news of any description but the more especially by bad news. The inhabitants of the village of Great Rooden did not differ from the rest of mankind in this respect and the evening of that day found many of the more curious sitting in the Lamb and Flag public house in the middle of the High Street. A regular visitor there would have found the bar unusually crowded for a Sunday evening in summer-time.

As well as the members of the parish there were also quite a number of people present from the Berebury Country Footpaths Society. They, having found the hostelry eminently satisfactory in the middle of the day, promptly repaired there again as soon as it was open in the evening to mull over the events of the afternoon. It was to them that Gordon Briggs was holding forth about the delights of the walk the Footpaths Society had missed that day.

"We'll do it next week," said one of his listeners, adding drily, "It won't have run away."

Briggs looked blank. A week might be a long time in politics; so it was in the investigation of murder.

"What are the police doing now?" asked someone else.

"They've gone up to Stanestede Farm," announced Len Hodge thickly. He was standing against the bar, well into his cups.

"Ted Mason tell you that, Len?" asked his drinking companion, who was called Arthur.

Hodge shook his head. "Poor old Ted's still seeing to everything at Pencombe." He took a long slow pull at his beer. "No, I heard the young copper being told to get on with it at Stanestede."

"That'll be Crosby," said Paul Hucham. The tall farmer had come down to the inn from Uppercombe Farm. He had been

128

listening attentively to Len Hodge's recital of the discovery in the farmyard. "I heard Inspector Sloan call him Crosby."

"He's rather nice," said Wendy Lamport. "I liked him."

"He's a policeman, isn't he?" growled Hodge. "There's no such animal as a nice policeman."

"Ted Mason's not so bad," volunteered his neighbour, "though I must say I'd like to know where he gets his cucumber seed."

"Seed!" snorted someone else. "You can say what you like, but I'm prepared to bet Ted doesn't use ordinary seed. Not for those cucumbers of his. If you ask me, he buys the chitted ones."

"What have they gone up to Stanestede for?" asked Briggs more pertinently.

"To ask Mrs. Ritchie how tall her husband was, that's for why," replied Len Hodge.

A little silence fell.

"My round," said a gallant soul into the conversational vacuum which followed this remark. It was always a good idea anyway to stand the drinks early rather than late. The man had learnt that in the army.

"'Bout how long would it be since anyone saw Mr. Ritchie then?" asked Arthur, finishing his glass and pushing it back to the landlord for a refill in one practised movement. "Same again, Vic, please."

"He hasn't been around since I don't know when," said someone else.

"Beginning of June, anyway," said Len Hodge.

"They do say," put in the landlord with a journalistic concern for protecting his sources, "that he went on Market Day."

"Young Jenkins didn't see him that morning at all," said a man standing against the bar. "Only on the Wednesday."

"And nobody's seen him since," said Arthur, resuming his glass without delay. "That I do know." He drew the top off the beer and added carefully, "Unless that's him up there on the roof."

"Gone to the mortuary," Hodge updated him, "for that doctor fellow they had up there for to have a proper look at him."

"A bad business all the same," said Paul Hucham heavily, "whoever it is. The sooner it's cleared up the better. Your governor'll be pretty put out, I daresay, Len."

"Stands to reason, doesn't it," said Hodge, suddenly becoming very taciturn indeed. The taciturnity might have been due to the beer; it might not.

Wendy Lamport shivered. She was there with her friend, Helen, drinking shandy. She said, "I still don't like to think about it."

"Don't, then," said Gordon Briggs, although it was actually the only thing that any of them could think—or talk—about that evening.

"No use running away from facts," said Hucham. He turned to the farmworker for agreement. "Is there, Len?"

Hodge plunged his face into his beer tankard before he spoke. "It all depends what you mean by facts."

Gordon Briggs, schoolmaster first, last and all the time, opened his mouth to begin a disquisition on what constituted a fact.

"Ah...," said Len Hodge's friend Arthur, infusing the expression with such overtones that Gordon Briggs was constrained to close his mouth again without having uttered a word.

"There's facts and facts, isn't there?" declared Hodge combatively.

It was the measure of the scowl on Hodge's face that Gordon Briggs did not even speak when the man made this contradictory statement. Two varieties of fact would most certainly not have been permitted in Mr. Briggs's class—but then his pupils were not, in the main, well over six feet tall, accustomed to hard physical work and standing against the bar in an attitude proclaiming a willingness to take on all comers.

The tall farmer from Uppercombe did not disagree with Len Hodge either. "It's a bad business whatever way you look at it," said Hucham.

Wendy Lamport looked troubled. "And it's not over yet, is it?" She looked round the circle of faces. "I mean, someone must have done it and we don't know who, do we?"

"Not yet, miss," said Arthur. He drank some of his beer and then said slowly, "Leastways, I don't—"

Hodge turned and began belligerently, "Now exactly what do you mean by that, Arthur Sellars?"

Even Gordon Briggs, remote and ineffectual schoolmaster, knew that when old friends started using surnames when speaking to each other there was trouble brewing. "What matters," said the schoolmaster in the tone which he used for quelling the third form, "is whether the police know, and if they don't, they'll soon find out."

"I do hope so," said Wendy Lamport, nervously fingering her shandy glass.

"Me, too," said her friend Helen. "I mean to say, it's not very nice to think about it, is it?"

In his day Gordon Briggs had taught for a whole English lesson on the abuse of the word "nice" as an adjective and any boy who used it in his essays could expect to find an astringent comment on the paucity of his vocabulary written in red ink in the margin. This evening he let it go by without a murmur. What happened today at Pencombe came in his mind into the category of pure Grand Guignol, and the bar of the Lamb and Flag was no place for a lecture on a popular eighteenth-century French puppet theatre specialising in the macabre and gruesome. Its similarity to Punch and Judy shows was another matter to be held over for a different setting. There was, as Gordon Briggs himself frequently observed, a time and a place for everything.

"If you ask me," said Wendy Lamport, staring fixedly into her glass, "there's something funny in Dresham Wood, too."

"Is there?" said Len Hodge, suddenly very casual.

"What makes you say that?" asked Paul Hucham, leaning forward attentively.

"You won't laugh, will you, if I tell you?"

Nobody laughed. They all waited instead, looking at her intently.

"I had such a funny feeling when we were going through the wood yesterday morning," she said.

"A funny feeling," repeated Hucham in the manner of an accomplished professional listener. It was one of the techniques of the psychiatrist's couch. Repeat what the last speaker has just said and they will go on and say more, was how the psychology textbooks put it.

"I told you about it, Gordon, didn't I?" she said, turning to Briggs. "When we came out of the wood yesterday."

Briggs nodded.

"What sort of funny feeling?" asked Hucham.

"That I was being watched."

Nobody said anything at all. That was a technique used by radio and television interviewers.

Wendy hurried on. "You know the feeling, don't you? I

can't explain it exactly but all the time I was in the wood I knew someone was looking at me."

"Did you tell the police about it, miss?" asked Len Hodge, his face muffled by his glass.

She shook her head.

"You can't tell the police about a feeling," said her friend Helen sturdily. "Feelings aren't evidence, are they?" It was a view shared by most magistrates and nearly all juries, and opened up a tempting by-path of discussion.

Wendy Lamport ignored it. "It wasn't only a feeling," she said.

All her listeners moved forward slightly, projecting increased interest in the finite.

"What was it, then?" asked Hodge, running his tongue over his lips.

"I saw a shoe by the path."

"A shoe?"

She nodded.

"A man's shoe?"

"Yes." She nodded again. "It came back to me this afternoon after—after they'd found what was on the roof—that I'd seen it yesterday, I mean," she went on a little incoherently, "lying by the path."

There was a general relaxation of tension in those round the bar.

"An old shoe doesn't amount to much, miss," said Hodge.

"There's always things like that in a wood," contributed Arthur.

"People throw things away," said Paul Hucham. "They dump stuff they don't want on my land too."

"It wasn't so much the shoe being there yesterday," went on Wendy slowly, "as its not being there today."

A certain tautness came back into the atmosphere.

"That was what I've just remembered, you see," she said. "That it had gone by the time we walked that way to Mr. Bailey's this afternoon."

"That's quite different," pronounced Paul Hucham firmly. "I think I should tell the police about that if I were you." He looked down at his watch and downed the last of his drink. "Well, I don't know about everybody else but I must be getting along. It's Monday tomorrow and there's work to be done in the morning. . . ."

So there was for them all but Len and Arthur were easily

persuaded into having another beer by Gordon Briggs and
the two girls seemed in no hurry to leave the comfort and
fellowship of the public house. The landlord had called
"Time, gentlemen, please" more than once before the bars of
the Lamb and Flag were quite emptied of people. Unfortunately
no one noticed the order in which the customers left. It
would have saved the police a lot of work if they had done so.

There was, of course, the usual flurry of car doors banging
and cheery calls of farewell before a country stillness settled
over the car-park. In the midsummer dim of night no one
noticed that there was still one car left there. There was no
one about either—until the next morning, that is—to see its
owner lying unconscious by the side of the car.

Wendy Lamport never knew what it was that had hit her.

FIFTEEN

•

Our ghostly enemy restrain

"What!" bellowed Superintendent Leeyes.

'Twas on a Monday morning, all right, but he wasn't dashing away with a smoothing iron. He was sitting at his desk in his office at Berebury Police Station wildly waving a report about in his fist. Detective Inspector Sloan had been summoned upon the instant.

"Who," demanded Leeyes, although it was all set out for him in writing, "has been found where?"

"Wendy Lamport," replied Sloan tautly. There was a hymn that he dimly remembered which began "Morning has broken. . . ." It was meant to herald the beginning of a glad day. Today wasn't a glad day.

"The girl who found the finger on Saturday," said Leeyes ominously.

"The girl," said Sloan astringently, "who was talking to all and sundry in the Lamb and Flag last night about there being something in the wood."

"That was obviously a very dangerous thing to do, Sloan, wasn't it?"

"We think she was simply hit on the head from behind," said Sloan.

Leeyes grunted. "Easy enough in the dark."

"She wasn't found until this morning." Sloan had started to piece his narrative together. "Pub people don't get up all that early."

"It's the late nights," agreed Leeyes. "Well?"

"She's still alive," reported Sloan.

"That's something," said Leeyes fervently.

"I've just come from the hospital." There had been a message from Dr. Dabbe, too, but he would have to wait. Sloan had gone to see the doctor of the living first. The duty house surgeon at the Berebury District General Hospital was a young man in his first year of finding out what medicine was really all about. Passing Wendy Lamport's distraught parents

134

in the corridor Sloan suddenly saw the attractions of forensic pathology very clearly. Those who practised it were protected from anxious relatives as well as living patients.

"Is she going to live?" growled Leeyes.

Sloan couldn't answer that. The house surgeon whom Sloan had spoken with had been altogether too guarded for his liking. The policeman, trained himself to be noncommittal, had been aware of much careful picking of words by the doctor. There were not a few unfinished sentences, too, and more than one chilling mention of the word "hope." When doctors started talking about there always being hope Sloan knew things were pretty bad.

"Or," continued Leeyes militantly, "is there going to be trouble with those infernal machines?"

Sloan winced. That was another complication. These days Death wasn't the only alternative to Life. There was a twilight area in between comprised of tubes and oxygen and ventilators and heart pumps. In *The Ballad of Reading Gaol* Oscar Wilde's doctor had said that death was but a Scientific Fact but it didn't seem to be even that any more. Not if what Sloan had heard was anything to go by. Not if you were on a life-support machine, that is.

"Not trouble, sir, exactly," he answered the superintendent with deliberation.

Wendy Lamport's doctor hadn't said that death was but a Scientific Fact at all. On the contrary. He had described death as a process, not an event. . . .

"Then he's never met a murderer, Sloan, has he?" said Leeyes flatly.

"No, sir. Probably not." Death being considered a process though at least explained some of the difficulties in diagnosing it these days. Sloan coughed. "The doctor says that if there are indications of brain death he'll—er—pull the plug out." He wondered if in time the phrase would succeed "kicking the bucket" and "going for a Burton."

"I hope he knows what he's doing," growled Leeyes.

"He's never seen an injury like Wendy Lamport's before," rejoined Sloan. The house surgeon had admitted as much: but then he was a very young man.

Leeyes grunted.

Sloan had taken a look at the girl himself, recumbent on a hospital pallet, but it hadn't told him anything more than he knew already. To all intents and purposes Wendy Lamport

was a lay figure suspended half-way between life and death.
He had stood at the bottom of her bed for a moment with the
house surgeon but it hadn't helped anything except his
resolve to bring whosoever had caused the injury to book.

"I've got a woman police constable sitting by her bed in
case she speaks," said Sloan. It was the sum total of all that
the police could do at this moment for Wendy Lamport.

Leeyes laid the paper he had been clutching down on his
desk. "I don't like it, Sloan," he said.

"No, sir."

"It puts us into a whole new ball game."

"Yes, sir." He cleared his throat. "I have to report that Mr.
and Mrs. Tom Mellot cannot be located at the present time—"

"You're looking for them though, aren't you, Sloan?" he
growled.

"Everyone is looking for them," replied Sloan with feeling.
He glanced down at his notebook and hurried on. "Various
South American countries with whom the United Kingdom
has no extradition treaties will neither confirm nor deny that
Ivor Harbeton is there."

"If," pronounced Leeyes, "neither the newspapers nor his
creditors could find him I don't think we shall." It was realism
that brought promotion, too.

"And, of course," went on Sloan doggedly, "we're trying to
establish where everyone was when the Lamb and Flag
closed last night."

"Everyone?" said Leeyes with a graphic gesture of his free
hand. "Who is everyone? Tell me that. . . ."

Sloan repressed a sigh. The superintendent had an absolute
gift for putting his finger on the sore point. He marshalled his
thoughts. "George Mellot—"

"Where was he?"

"Taking the dog for a walk," said Sloan hollowly.

Leeyes grunted.

"Constable Mason," said Sloan, "was still on duty at Pencombe
Farm. He says Mrs. Mellot didn't leave the building. He
didn't," added Sloan, "get away until after closing-time." This
was something which clearly rankled with Ted Mason. "And
Sam Bailey and his wife at Lowercombe—"

"Yes?" said Leeyes alertly. "It's their wood, isn't it, that the
girl had been talking about? Dresham or something? You're
searching the wood, aren't you, Sloan?"

"Yes, sir, the men are on their way there now." He cleared

his throat. "Sam Bailey went to bed early, or so they both say."

"Well, they would, woudn't they?"

"Mrs. Bailey," Sloan forged on, "says she went for a little stroll before she went to bed as it had been such a hot day. She says her husband was asleep when she got back."

"Could a woman have done it?"

"With the right weapon, sir," said Sloan uneasily. "I think she could."

"So you are looking for two things now, are you, Sloan?"

"Two, sir?" echoed Sloan.

"Do I have to spell everything out?" he said irritably. "Two, Sloan. What the girl was hit with and what the head of the body was cut off with." Gordon Briggs, the schoolmaster, would have had something to say about ending sentences with prepositions but Sloan couldn't have put it better himself.

"Yes, sir," he responded readily enough. Dr. Dabbe had told them yesterday exactly what to look for in connection with the head. Or disconnection. Something heavy and sharp and slightly curved, he had said.

"You can kill two birds with one stone, then, can't you, Sloan?" said Leeyes felicitously, "and look for them both at the same time."

"Won't keep you a moment, Inspector," called out Dr. Dabbe as Sloan and Crosby entered the mortuary.

Sloan ground his teeth. It was always the way when he was in a hurry.

"I'm just finishing a George Bernard Shaw case," announced Dr. Dabbe.

"Pardon, Doctor?" said Sloan, a little startled.

"A Doctor's Dilemma," said the consultant pathologist with a cheeriness wholly unsuited to his surroundings. "I'm the only person, you know, who can tell 'em whether they had been treating the patient for the right thing."

"I hadn't thought of that."

"And whether they did that properly," said the pathologist as a rider. "Medical audits are a bit of a vogue at the moment."

Crosby pricked up his ears at the mention of the word "audit." "Old accountants never die," he chanted. "They just lose their balance."

"And you, Doctor," said Sloan, manfully rising above this,

"now tell the other doctors whether they were right or wrong
in their diagnosis?" It seemed a bit late to Sloan to be of any
help: like a public enquiry after a riot.

"Bless you, Inspector," said Dr. Dabbe, pulling off the
surgical cap which covered his hair, "I've always done that.
That's what post-mortems are for."

"Well, then . . ."

"What's new," said the pathologist, undoing his rubber
apron, "is that now the doctors tell each other."

"Confession is good for the soul," observed Crosby
sententiously.

Sloan said nothing. He was possessing his own soul in
patience at the moment, waiting for Dr. Dabbe to come to
their particular case, where the surgery had been distinctly
amateur. It was different in the police force anyway. There
your superior officer told you if you had been wrong—and
pretty smartly. He usually told everyone else, too, about your
mistakes. . . .

"It might be good for the soul," Dr. Dabbe countered
Crosby, "but it's bad for confidence."

"What about truth?" Detective Inspector Sloan, well brought
up by his mother, was stirred into speech in spite of himself.

"The practice of medicine," declared Dr. Dabbe didactical-
ly, "has nothing to do with truth."

"Pardon, Doctor?"

"The practice of medicine is a purely empirical exercise,
Sloan. Truth doesn't come into it."

Sloan drew breath to answer.

Dr. Dabbe forestalled him. "It is only here in the post-
mortem room that truth and medicine come together."

"When it's all over bar the shouting," protested Sloan.

"Nobody should expect perfection this side of the grave,"
said Dr. Dabbe with a solemnity that Sloan found himself
quite unable to measure.

"Here we suffer grief and pain," chimed in Crosby. "Across
the road it's just the same."

Sloan gave up. "About the skeleton on the barn roof," he
said weakly.

"Ah, your chappie . . ." The pathologist stripped off his
surgical gown and canted it adroitly into a basket for soiled
linen. "I can tell you now that decapitation was almost
certainly the cause of death."

"That doesn't happen every day," said Sloan.

"No."

"There may have been a reason for removing the head, too," said Sloan slowly, thinking aloud.

"Yes, I think that's a proper inference." The pathologist stroked his chin. "I don't think a psychopath would have concealed the body so carefully. They don't care, you know."

Sloan did know. There were two sorts of Untouchables—those at the bottom of the caste system and those who remained untouched by human feeling. He said, "Did it—can you tell—was it taken off while the person was on the roof or before?"

"Before," said the pathologist without hesitation. "There wouldn't have been enough purchase for anyone to stand on the sloping roof and swing anything down on something well below them with the force that decapitation would have needed."

"Besides," agreed Sloan, "there would have been footmarks."

"There weren't any footmarks," said Crosby.

"Then," said the pathologist, "I assume that the head came off on terra firma."

"So it wasn't an afterthought," remarked Crosby with a perfectly straight face.

Sloan turned to Dr. Dabbe in despair. "If you had a skull, Doctor, you could superimpose a photograph of a person over a photograph of the skull, couldn't you?" The observation sounded to Sloan like one of those jokes children made amongst themselves. If we had some bacon we could have bacon and eggs—if we had some eggs.

"I could indeed," said the pathologist warmly.

"If the cap fits...," began Crosby from the sidelines.

"And if we had some clothes," said Sloan heavily, "we should have known better where to start looking for a photograph."

"'The apparel oft proclaims the man.'" Dr. Dabbe quoted Polonius, reaching as he did so for the jacket of his own well-cut, professionally dark and striped suit.

"Clothes are a dead give-away," interposed Crosby wittily.

"That will have been why he was naked, I expect," said Sloan. Of course William Shakespeare had put it better. He always did.

"The problem, from your point of view," said the pathologist pontifically, "appears to be primarily one of identification.

All the steps taken by whoever put him on the roof point in that direction."

"Quite so," agreed Sloan, although he was silently following a very different train of thought himself. In artists' representations of hell people were always depicted as naked. He'd noticed it on those half-circle things above church doors whose name sounded like something to do with the eardrum. It would come back to him presently. Hell, with its naked people, was always on the sinister side. On the other side would be heaven. Angels always came up clothed. He supposed there would be an explanation for that if he looked for it. Sigmund Freud, if nobody else, would have had a suggestion. Only one, of course. Tympanum, that was what the half circle in the church was called. . . .

"And the problem from my point of view," said the pathologist, neatly separating church and state in Sloan's mind.

"Yes?"

"Establishing the cause of death if it wasn't decapitation," said Dr. Dabbe, "and helping you towards identification."

Sloan nodded. That was the doctor's exact province.

"I can't help you any further with either, Sloan," continued Dabbe. "The answer may lie in the head, of course, to both, and that may have been the reason for its removal."

"We're looking for it now, Doctor."

"A sort of Salome in reverse," said Crosby, moving to one side to get a specimen case out of his line of vision. "Funny sort of souvenirs you keep in here, Doctor. It isn't cauliflower cheese, is it? That white furry stuff over there? No, I thought not."

"Talking about heads, Doctor," intervened Sloan quickly, "there's something you should know." He told the pathologist about Wendy Lamport's fractured skull.

He looked grave. "That's bad, Sloan. It means that time isn't on your side, doesn't it?"

"If we hadn't found the skeleton," said Sloan, "she would have been all right." It was something that was beginning to worry him. He didn't know if that was what was called lateral thinking or not. He never even knew whether it was right to replace Fate or Predestination with coincidence or even a mad randomness. His grandmother had always added the proviso "If I'm spared" when making an engagement—just in case.

"Disposing of the body is the eternal problem of all murderers," he said.

"No," said Dr. Dabbe. "No, Sloan, it's not."

"No, Doctor? What is, then?"

"Eternity itself," said the pathologist-turned-philosopher solemnly.

"Ah."

"Dante," said Dr. Dabbe, picking up something that looked remarkably like a stainless steel chisel and pointing it at Sloan the better to punctuate his remarks, "had Julius Caesar's murderers devoured eternally by Satan in the bottommost pit of hell."

"That's different," objected Sloan. The Last Judgement might be a sort of catch-all for police officers who had been unsuccessful in solving a crime, but it didn't absolve a detective from doing his duty.

"Not really...."

"I shall be quite happy to settle for the dock of the Crown Court at Calleford," said Sloan firmly. That was as far as a simple police officer needed to go: everything else could safely be left to St. Peter. "Come along, Crosby, there's work to be done...."

"Where to, sir?" asked Detective Constable Crosby, tumbling into the police car. He liked driving fast cars fast.

"Great Rooden," said Sloan with a distinct sense of relief. Great Rooden was where the action had been and there was where the police should be: not in police stations or hospitals or mortuaries.

"Great Rooden it is," said Crosby, engaging gear.

"Lowercombe Farm first," said Sloan. They would go back to the Lamb and Flag too, and Pencombe Farm, but a visit to Lowercombe Farm came first.

"We're on our way," said Crosby unnecessarily. The police car was in top gear already.

"Dresham Wood, to be exact," said Sloan. Other policemen from F Division, led by Constable Ted Mason on account of his local knowledge, had already been searching it for some time. The first thing that Sloan had done after hearing about the attack on Wendy Lamport had been to order men there. He hadn't known what to tell them to look for: he had just asked to be told if there was anything there that wasn't usual in a wood. Ten to one a comedian would report a great crested tit and expect him to laugh and he wouldn't. . . .

"To the woods, to the woods," chanted Crosby joyously.

"Crosby, it may have escaped your notice," interposed Sloan mildly, "that one of Traffic Division's unmarked cars is right behind you."

"Lawks 'a' mercy," croaked Crosby. The speed of the police car fell appreciably.

"I don't have to remind you," went on Sloan smoothly, "that Inspector Harpe takes a very strict view of unnecessary speeding by police vehicles." Inspector Harpe was the head of Berebury's Traffic Division and was known throughout the Calleshire force as Happy Harry because he had never been seen to smile. On his part Inspector Harpe maintained that in Traffic Division there had never been anything yet at which to even twitch a lip.

"Yes, sir," said Crosby with unexpected docility.

Sloan made no further comment, but sat back in his seat and tried to marshal his thoughts instead.

It wasn't easy.

He stared unseeingly out of the window of the car as the Calleshire countryside went by. The summer scene was a beautiful one, but his mind's eye was centred on an innocent girl hovering between life and death in a hospital bed and someone out at Great Rooden prepared to kill not once but twice and he—they—still didn't even know why, let alone who. He didn't even have the beginnings of a picture in his mind of the sort of person the murderer might be.

Ruthless, of course. That went without saying. Pitilessness was one characteristic common to all killers.

Strong. Even with a fork-lift tractor getting a body up and onto a roof took strength.

Clever. The barn roof had been a good place to hide a victim. Sloan didn't doubt for a moment that the victim's head too was somewhere nobody would think of looking. They would have to search for that when they had finished going through the wood. And after that there was the weapon which had been used to hit Wendy Lamport to look for, to say nothing of the instrument that had separated the first victim's head from his shoulders.

Even the catalogue didn't include finding who it was that had killed the man on the roof, whoever he was. Who he was

was something else they didn't know. All in all the police hadn't made a lot of progress to date.

It transpired that Crosby, too, had been thinking. "I suppose, sir, that that attack on the girl last night lets Tom Mellot out."

"I don't see why," objected Sloan sourly. It rankled a little that Tom Mellot hadn't been found. A man, his wife, two children and a white Sealyham terrier with a black patch over one ear shouldn't have been able to be swallowed up into the background quite so easily. "He could be anywhere."

Crosby hunched his shoulders over the wheel as they passed out of the thirty-mile-an-hour limit. "It would have narrowed the field, that's all, if we could have counted him out."

"Narrowed the field," echoed Sloan richly. "Narrowed the field!" He countered simile with simile. "Do you realise, Crosby, that we don't even know the names of the runners yet?"

Crosby took this literally. "George Mellot."

"His barn, of course," conceded Sloan.

"Len Hodge."

"He would call it his fork-lift tractor," said Sloan drily. "And it was his fight."

"Sam Bailey and his wife," said Crosby.

"Their wood," agreed Sloan. Time would tell what was in their wood.

"Andrina Ritchie."

"Her husband gone," said Sloan. "I must say she sounded as if she would have killed him if she could."

"Tom Mellot."

"His firm," said Sloan.

"He'd have known his way around the farmyard, all right," said Crosby. "He was born there."

"And Len Hodge would have helped him, I expect," said Sloan. "He'd known him all his life, remember." Those were the people you turned to in real need. The early companions on life's journey were linked by a bond of time and place. When it came to the crunch they didn't let you down. Women were inclined to joke about the old school tie, but it was a bond for all that. It didn't have to be a silk one with a crest and a Latin motto on it either. The early association was what counted, be it the council school at the end of the street not named after anyone at all, founded like as not by the

stroke of a committee's pen as a consequence of some reforming
Act of Parliament, or a Gothic pile set up by an English king
in a moment spared from battle or politicking with the
French. It didn't matter.

Or a village school that everyone's son went to.

"Paul Hucham?" said Crosby tentatively.

"He seems clean." Sloan knew better than to absolve
anyone on those grounds alone.

"He was in the Lamb and Flag last night."

"He can lift a sheep," said Sloan absently, remembering his
visit to Uppercombe Farm. "Not that that makes him a
murderer..."

The search-party had found something in Dresham Wood.
Sloan could tell from the whole mien of the man who walked
towards him as they arrived. Constable Mason wasn't able to
keep the satisfaction out of his voice either as he reported to
Sloan.

SIXTEEN

•

Nor phantoms of the night appear

Superintendent Leeyes's response was dampening.

"It doesn't sound a lot to me," he said down the telephone line from Berebury Police Station to Sam Bailey's farmhouse at Great Rooden.

"Someone," insisted Sloan, "has been living in Dresham Wood."

All the signs were there. Police Constable Mason had taken Sloan to see them. There was a thicket not far from the water's edge that had first attracted the attention of the police. A few leafy branches had been bent over some bushes to provide a sort of shelter and round about it were more signs of human habitation. Grass had been squashed down where someone had lain and twigs snapped off. . . .

"Found a camp-fire, have you?" grunted Leeyes.

There had been no burnt-out remains of a fire. Whoever had been living in the wood had not cooked food nor seen a winter out in the open.

"Footprints," replied Sloan succinctly. Even now a police constable was making a plaster cast of what looked like a size eight man's shoe, noticeably down at heel. "And litter . . ."

There were no dustbins in Dresham Wood and it seemed that no one could live without creating debris. Archaeologists fell upon Roman rubbish dumps with delight for the information they gave.

So did detectives.

"Not just someone camping out?" enquired Leeyes.

"Someone living rough, I should say," said Sloan judiciously.

"A stake-out?"

"We found some food," said Sloan, cradling the telephone receiver between his ear and his shoulder the better to be able to turn over the pages of his notebook. He cleared his throat and said with deliberation, "Proper food."

The line crackled. "What exactly do you mean by that, Sloan?"

"Properly cooked food," elaborated Sloan. "The end of a

joint of beef. Pieces of fruit-cake. Home-made fruit-cake," he
added pointedly. Constable Mason, part-time gourmand, had
been most insistent about the good quality of the fruit-cake:
had said it was important. And so it was.

Leeyes grunted. "Anything else?"

"Bottles," said Sloan.

"Ah . . ."

"They weren't obvious, of course," said Sloan. "They were
tucked away."

"They usually are," said Leeyes.

"Even when there is a dustbin," agreed Sloan. The disposal of bottles was a perennial problem for real drinkers.

"It's not a crime to live rough," observed Leeyes, "and it
doesn't mean that he—whoever he is—is a murderer."

"It's a funny thing to do, all the same," continued Sloan
stoutly, bolstered by that piece in the Bible about foxes
having holes and the birds of the air having nests.

"You didn't get him, I suppose?" said Leeyes mordantly.

"No," said Sloan, adding a rather belated "sir." It was
marvellous how the superintendent always managed to touch
a raw spot. Ted Mason's search-party had done all the right
things—like throwing a cordon round the wood before they
went into it. Nothing, the village constable had insisted,
could have popped out without being caught. No more, he
had said, than a rabbit could have escaped a harvest shoot,
not if it had taken refuge in the centre of a field, that is. In
the end the reaper and binder—only that had got some
newfangled name now and it wasn't even called a harvester
any more—cut down all the cover and the rabbits didn't have
anywhere else to hide.

"So, Sloan, the bird had flown by the time you'd got there,"
said Leeyes, contriving not only to touch a raw spot but to
put his underling in the wrong at the same time. That was a
gift, too.

Sloan took a resolution about not being too defensive.
"There was no one in the wood by the time it was searched,"
he said without any inflexion at all.

"And no one knows anything about anything, I suppose,"
said Leeyes testily.

"Sam Bailey says he doesn't," said Sloan. "I've just interviewed
him." The old farmer was behaving exactly like James Forsyte
and carrying on about nobody telling him anything.

"Hrrrrmmmpph," said Leeyes.

"And Mrs. Bailey," reported Sloan, "left by car before the search-party arrived for Calleford. Or so her husband says. She didn't say when she would be back."

Leeyes grunted. "And what has Len Hodge got to say for himself?"

"The Great Rooden fire brigade was called out to a barn said to be on fire over at Easterbrook. That's to the north of the parish," added Sloan, "but it's quite a way from here. Leading fireman Hodge was at the wheel of the tender and the crew hasn't come back yet."

"Said to be on fire?" Leeyes picked up kernels as quickly as a sow after acorns.

"False alarm, malicious intent," said Sloan neatly. Every service had its own short-speak and the fire brigade was no exception.

"Funny time for fun and games like that, first thing Monday morning," grunted Leeyes.

"They think it's a boy playing truant," said Sloan. There was a world of work and school—a better-regulated world than the one in which Sloan lived and had his being—in which work began on Monday morning and finished—for better or worse—on Friday afternoon.

"So we don't even know if Hodge knows about the girl, Wendy Lamport, being found yet?"

"That's difficult to say," answered Sloan slowly. In remote villages like Great Rooden it was impossible to know who knew what. It was akin to working in a fog, not knowing what was going on around you and not being able to see who was talking to whom. And sometimes, too, hearing things and not knowing from whence they came...

"Or about the wood being searched," said Leeyes.

"No," agreed Sloan. One thing, though, was certain about villages and that was that news spread like wildfire. He, a detective inspector from the far-away town, wasn't going to be silly enough to say who knew what in Great Rooden. He was prepared to bet, all the same, that everyone in Great Rooden knew that he, Sloan, was back in the parish and that Dresham Wood had been searched.

"He'll hear soon enough if he doesn't," said Leeyes realistically.

"Yes, sir." What Sloan would like to have known was how many people knew that someone—a man, if the footprint was anything to go by—had been living in the wood.

And for how long.

He'd told them to leave the bottles where they were. A biologist might be able to look underneath them and say how long they'd been lying there. Mould told the experts quite a lot as well. Crosby was taking some fingerprints from one of the bottles at this moment. He'd found them round the neck. Whoever had been living in the wood had not troubled with a glass.

"This mysterious stranger that Len Hodge had a fight with, Sloan—"

"I shall be talking to him about that," promised Sloan, "as soon as I can get hold of him. And about one or two other things as well."

"What about the Mellots?" said Leeyes. He was like a terrier with its teeth into the seat of somebody's trousers: he wasn't going to let go.

"I'm going there now," said Sloan, "but I'm prepared to bet that they'll say that they don't know anything about anything, too."

"Clams," agreed Leeyes reflectively, "don't have anything on people in villages. Touch 'em and they close up."

Somewhere at the back of his mind was something Sloan had once read and remembered. It had been written by that prescient fellow who had written about 1984 and all that. "Those who have the beans," he quoted neatly, "seldom spill them."

Detective Constable Crosby was stowing the fingerprint gear back into the police car when Sloan emerged from Lowercombe Farm, blinking a little in the sunlight. It had been dark and cool inside the ancient farmhouse. Old Sam Bailey had been pacing up and down all the while, anxiety manifesting itself as crossness. He followed Sloan outside now rather like an old dog with nothing else to think about.

"What shall I do next?" he asked rather pathetically.

"Try to think of places where your wife might have gone," commanded Sloan crisply, "and ring her up and ask her to come back home."

Talking to Mrs. Elsie Bailey had become suddenly very relevant. He hadn't forgotten that there had been leaf-mould on her shoes yesterday afternoon; had it only been yesterday afternoon? It seemed aeons ago. If he, Sloan, had acted more promptly yesterday afternoon he might have saved Wendy

Lamport from being injured. He braced himself mentally: policemen had to live with such thoughts just as doctors did. If you couldn't, you didn't make the grade. Detective inspectors and general practitioners were the survivors.

The grizzled farmer nodded and made his way back indoors looking more bewildered than ever, his pepperiness suddenly evaporated.

"We're going over to the Mellots' next," said Sloan to Crosby, "to see what they've got to say for themselves."

"A proper Teddy bears' picnic, that was, in the wood," remarked Crosby, slamming the car boot lid shut.

"Yes," responded Sloan briefly, his mind on something else.

"'If you go down to the woods today,'" chanted the constable, "'you're sure of a big surprise.'"

"No," said Sloan seriously. "We knew all along that there was something in the wood. What we didn't know was what it was."

"A man," said Crosby. "Not much doubt about that now."

"He'd been there for quite a while," said Sloan. "All the evidence points to that."

"The bottles and things," agreed Crosby largely.

"Doesn't that strike you as strange?" said Sloan.

"I've never liked the idea of living rough myself," said Crosby, opening the driver's door.

"We're walking to Pencombe," said Sloan.

"Oh." He shut the door.

"A man," said Sloan, returning to the matter at hand, "has been living rough in Dresham Wood probably for several weeks and yet Ted Mason, who is said by everyone to know all about Great Rooden, didn't know about him. Doesn't that strike you as strange?"

"I thought Ted's beat was so quiet he could hear the grass growing," agreed Crosby.

"Exactly." Sloan tightened his lips. "It's as funny as Len Hodge having a stand-up fight with a total stranger."

"You don't have total strangers in villages like this," concurred Crosby, falling into step beside Sloan in more ways than one.

"A stranger who is said not to have been seen since."

"We've got a spare stranger," offered Crosby in melancholy tones. "Over at the mortuary."

"All we know," persisted Sloan, "is that a month ago a man was killed and last night a girl was badly injured."

"That's not a coincidence," said Crosby.

"No," said Sloan reflectively, "I don't think it is. Although I must say I don't see the connection just at the moment."

"I wonder what would have happened if that crow hadn't dropped the finger just where it did," said Crosby.

"Wendy Lamport would be at work this morning for one thing," said Sloan soberly, "and not lying at death's door." Justice was a purely abstract concept and was something quite different.

"It's all a bit difficult, though, isn't it?" said the detective constable.

"Complaining before you get to the stile, Crosby?" said Sloan appositely as the road between the two farms came into view.

"We still don't know anything for certain," insisted the constable. He didn't like walking and it brought out the worst in him.

"Just that harm was done to Wendy Lamport," said Sloan, "and that about a month ago an unknown man was killed. That's about all we know."

"We aren't even sure it was murder," grumbled Crosby. "The doctor won't put that in black and white."

"The body was decapitated and placed out of sight."

"Good enough for a jury, I suppose," said Crosby, capitulating on this particular point. "They won't go for an accident or misadventure."

"And left naked," said Sloan, putting a foot on the stile at the beginning of the footpath to Pencombe. Naked Truth he knew all about. She appeared in a famous picture. Naked Villainy presumably had a long heritage too. He didn't know if there was any connection, but he did know that the nakedness would weigh heavily with the jury. So would the decapitation. The command "off with his head" was something usually reserved for the enigmatic world of *Alice in Wonderland* and Tudor politics—not the contemporary English rural scene. Naked men didn't really belong either. . . .

Crosby scuffed at a stone with his shoe.

"After which," continued Sloan steadily, "nothing happened at all until the finger was found."

That was interesting in itself. There had been no hue and cry, no missing person reported, no pleas of the "Come home, all forgiven" variety, no welcoming lamp burning in the window at eventide. . . .

Presumably the waters had closed over someone as surely as if they had never been—and yet that didn't make sense either. Someone sufficiently important to be disposed of with such care must have been very much in someone else's way. It was also, it suddenly occurred to Sloan, a case of the victim being someone whose death didn't need to be known about to achieve the outcome the murderer wanted.

Or murderers.

They mustn't, Sloan reminded himself, forget that it wasn't only in the plays of William Shakespeare that murderers came up in pairs. It happened in real life, too. At the very least whoever put the body on the roof of the barn at Pencombe would have needed a look-out. Unless it had been the Mellots, of course. And if it hadn't been the Mellots then they would have to have been got out of the way by somebody.

And if it hadn't been Len Hodge so would he.

To say nothing of the dog.

If the Mellots and Len Hodge had both been got out of the way then, supposed Sloan, it wouldn't have mattered very much if the dog had barked because then there wouldn't have been anyone there to hear it. In his view this did not mean that the sound had not occurred—although it had been on this very point that he had parted intellectual company with the science master at school. Sound did not exist, the old dominie had declared, unless there was an ear to hear it. Sound was merely a series of waves emanating from an action and pulsating through the atmosphere. It was the receiving ear that turned those waves into sound.

"Pencombe's farther away than it looks, isn't it?" remarked Crosby mundanely.

"The walk will do you good," responded Sloan unfeelingly. "Besides, it's giving us time to think." Police action was, of course, taking place as well. There was an unmarked police car shadowing leading fireman Len Hodge and the Great Rooden fire brigade over at Easterbrook and every policeman in Calleshire was on the lookout for Mrs. Elsie Bailey and her car. Every force in the country was on the alert for Mr. and Mrs. Tom Mellot, two small children, and a white Sealyham terrier with a black patch over its left ear.

"I can't think and walk," complained Crosby.

"That's a pity," he said with more than a little acerbity,

"because there's quite a lot for us to think about." The plural pronoun was singularly generous, he thought. To date Crosby didn't seem to have done any real thinking at all.

"The finger being found was a bit of bad luck for whoever put the body on the roof, anyway," said Crosby.

"And for Wendy Lamport," Sloan reminded him. There might be a message at any moment from the hospital.

Crosby kicked at another stone. "It's not something where death has to be proved or the body wouldn't have been hidden. It must have been someone who could just disappear."

"That's true." Sloan nodded approvingly. The aphorism "Where's there's a will, there's a way" could be construed in more than one fashion. And "will" could be written "will" with very sinister overtones indeed. "It doesn't appear," he concluded prosaically, "to be an inheritance matter."

Crosby wrinkled his brow. "All that trouble with the furnishing firm stopped a bit suddenly, didn't it?"

"The heat was off as soon as Ivor Harbeton disappeared," assented Sloan. "That was when the take-over fell through." What he really could have done with was a quiet chat with someone who knew about these things. Shocks and stares weren't his cup of tea: he had been brought up to believe them to be one stage removed from the gaming tables at Monte Carlo and nothing had happened to him in later life to make him change this view.

"The timing wasn't all that far out," said Crosby.

"It was dead right," said Sloan soberly. What he could not understand was why the entire police force of the United Kingdom could not lay their hands on Tom Mellot, his wife, two children and a dog.

"The timing was dead right for when Martin Ritchie took off as well," pointed out Crosby helpfully. A man was on his way to Stanestede Farm to check on the size of his shoes.

"Pity his wife threw his letter away," said Sloan. Circumstantial evidence always helped, especially when real evidence was hard to come by. And the making of marks on paper with pen and pencil was one of the most revealing actions a human being could make. There were those who could read more into handwriting than a biologist into a drop of pond water. It was just as well the study of calligraphy was a new science. Medieval graphologists would have soon been made bonfires of for witchcraft.

"She seems to be managing all right without him at the farm," offered Crosby.

"Spiders eat their husbands and still do well," said Sloan briskly. To his way of thinking militant feminists advanced all the wrong arguments.

The two policemen turned off the footpath and walked through the farmyard towards the back door of Pencombe Farm. Crosby jerked a finger in the direction of the barn roof as they did so. "Penny plain or twopence coloured?" he said. "You pays your money and you takes your choice."

"It's blood money, though, that you're paying with, don't forget," said Sloan. "That's the trouble. . . ."

Police Constable Ted Mason was feeling the heat in more ways than one. The temperature was rising steadily as the morning advanced. This sort of weather did not suit a man of his stature. The pressure of work which he was experiencing at the same time was all the more unwelcome for being unaccustomed. No one could have described Constable Mason as someone who was addicted to adrenaline.

He had been put in charge of the search for the instrument which might have been used to remove a head from a body—with a strong rider that he also apply himself to thinking of where a head, too, might have been hidden, "seeing how," Detective Inspector Sloan had added, "he was supposed to know every inch of his patch."

Neither task appealed to a man of his temperament. One required action and the other thought. Both were anathema to Constable Mason. His working life had been centred round the skilful referral to higher authority of anything involving any effort. Knotty problems arising in Great Rooden soon found themselves dispatched to the substation at Almstone. In the nature of things this was staffed by a series of young, ambitious—and newly promoted—sergeants, keen to show the powers that be at police headquarters how good they were at dealing with difficult matters. Points on which they were able to demonstrate their mastery of police law were sometimes even positively welcomed.

On the other hand anything that had been really likely to interfere seriously with the growing of prize cabbages Ted Mason had stamped on himself and forgotten to report.

With some good cause he had long ago decided that civil rights were a purely urban nicety and he had remained untroubled by them. Essentially rural devices like man-traps might be illegal and putting the villain in the stocks no longer a fashionable punishment, but the public pillory still existed in modern guise and Ted Mason had no hesitation in using it as a weapon. A threat to tell the world at large and the village of Great Rooden in particular—and for some the two were indivisible—about a breach of tribal behaviour kept many a petty law-breaker toeing the line. For those who had no fear of neighbours' tongues—and were thus almost beyond redemption—he devised more condign punishment.

Only when he couldn't think of a way of making the punishment fit the crime did Ted Mason invoke the due processes of the law. He was thus much less worried than most when the courts couldn't match the two either.

He was, in short, a believer in the white-glove treatment rather than the kid-glove variety.

As a very young constable Edward Mason had once been drafted from Calleshire to London for ceremonial duty. A uniform preternaturally spick and span had been embellished by a pair of white gloves. His training days were still fresh in his memory at the time and he remembered having been told that there had been an ancient custom for judges to be given a pair of gloves before a trial, together with a nosegay to keep the plague or something at bay. He had vaguely associated the gloves with this and had started to put them on.

"Wait a minute, wait a minute," growled the sergeant in charge. "They're not for wearing, lad. They're for carrying."

Constable Mason had stammered his apologies.

"Up from the country, are you?" The sergeant, who had been of the old school, had winked mightily. "Now hold them out and I'll show you a trick or two."

Mason had obediently held the white gloves out in front of him while the sergeant had filled the fingers with small steel ball-bearings.

"Right, lad. Now you hold those gloves in your right hand, see? And if you have any trouble with anyone in the crowd just give them a flick with those gloves and they won't forget it in a hurry. And," he added meaningfully, "should the television cameras or anyone else with fancy ideas about the police happen to see you doing it, there won't be any trouble afterwards, see?"

Constable Ted Mason had not only seen but had understood and remembered. He had long ago forgotten the event that had taken him to the capital. He had never forgotten the loaded white gloves....

Neither the Mason theory nor practice of policing was much help to him at this moment, though. He stood at the entrance to Dresham Wood now, a mass of indecision. There were men at his beck and call but he did not know where to tell them to start looking.

An instrument suitable for removing a head might be anywhere. So, if it came to that, might be the head.

Long grass would conceal anything at this time of the year—which didn't help.

And he didn't even know exactly what they were supposed to be looking for except that whatever it was it would have to have been man enough for the job.

Which didn't get him very far.

Automatically economical of effort, he thought before he moved.

It was the village butcher's shop which first came to mind. Hubert Wilkinson's was one of the old-fashioned variety. His name-board still proclaimed him as a butcher and grazier and time was when he had killed his own meat, but Hubert Wilkinson hung his knives up in the shop-window for all to see. If any one of them had been missing for so much as an hour, he, Ted Mason, would have heard all about it.

Somebody else who would have had a tool that would have taken off a head with ease was the old lengthman who used to keep the grass verges of the roadside cut, but he had been replaced by a gang of men from the County Council. They descended on Great Rooden once a year and did a botched job with an undiscriminating machine. The man who knew every culvert and gulley had been pensioned off and the village was the poorer for it.

Ted Mason dismissed the garage from his mind, too. Their tools weren't sharp. Even when it had been a forge, the tools of the transport trade had been stout and blunt.

He didn't allow his mind to dwell on the local doctor either, for all that he did have instruments that were sharp enough for the job. Doctors had easier ways of disposing of bodies than of humping them up onto barn roofs.

There was always Jimmie, the wood-spoiler, of course. Carpenters had saws. He would send a man to inspect Jimmie's saws.

The minion duly dispatched, Ted Mason continued to

think. Next he did what an old mentor of his had often advised and put himself in the other fellow's shoes. He tried to imagine himself with a body on his hands whose head he wanted off. He would obviously look near at hand first and for something that would not lead the trail straight back to him.

That meant using an instrument that belonged to some-body else; double bluff was for a more considered crime than this, he thought. It wasn't something for country constables to be worrying about anyway. What he was looking for was something that either would not be missed or had been replaced after use.

Police Constable Ted Mason was not an academic man and distinctions between pure and applied thought would have been lost upon him, but it was not all that long before he reached the conclusion that a search of Sam Bailey's old barn at Lowercombe Farm would do no harm.

And it was not long after that when he found an old implement that had once been used for topping sugar-beet.

It was by no means as dry and dusty as the other old tools beside it in the barn.

SEVENTEEN

•

The quick and the dead

There was something new and fancy in psychiatric circles called transactional analysis. Detective Inspector Sloan had read about it from time to time in such police journals as kept an eye on what trick cyclists were up to. It made him more conscious of the quality of the exchange he had now with George and Meg Mellot.

There was a formality about his interview with them that had been absent before. It added a new dimension to this particular interface between the officers of the law and John Citizen and his wife.

Sloan's first question had been a simple one. Even so it had provoked a visible shudder in Meg Mellot and clearly took George Mellot by surprise.

"The size of Tom's shoes?" echoed the farmer. "No, of course I don't know what size shoe Tom took. Why should I?" He turned to his wife. "Do you, Meg?"

She shook her head mutely.

Detective Inspector Sloan made a note. An ambitious young Spanish-speaking policeman in London might well get his fabada today after all. "Right, sir, then may we come back to the take-over bid for Mellot's Furnishings?"

George Mellot ran a tongue over dry lips and said wearily, "If you wish."

"When your father died and your brother took his portion—"

"No," said George Mellot.

"No?"

"Tom didn't take his portion," said George Mellot, "and he wasn't a prodigal son or anything like that. Tom just wasn't cut out to be a farmer."

"He couldn't stand the waiting, Inspector," put in Meg Mellot a little timidly.

Sloan turned to her for elucidation. "Waiting?"

There were two schools of thought in police circles. One was that you got more out of interviewing a husband and wife

157

together and the other was that you extracted more from each
separately. Detective Inspector Sloan took the more pragmat-
ic view that it all depended on the husband and wife.

"Farmers have to take the long view," she explained
awkwardly. "Sometimes they have to wait for years and years
to see the results of their work. It's not an overnight affair."

"Tom likes wheeling and dealing," amplified George Mellot.
"He enjoys having everything—er—instant, so to speak."

"So...," said Sloan steadily.

"So Tom went into business."

"With his share of your father's estate?" Business, conceded Sloan silently, called for everything instant—especially
judgements.

"Not exactly," temporised the farmer.

"How then?"

"It was all very well in the Bible," said Mellot tangentially,
"this taking off with your portion. I daresay all they had to do
was to divide the flock of sheep into two."

"Jacob and his sheep," said Sloan intelligently, "of another
colour."

Detective Constable Crosby stirred. "Have you heard," he
asked chattily, "about the man who practised animal husband-
ry until they found out and stopped him?"

Nobody took any notice of him.

The farmer frowned. "It isn't like it was in the Bible any more."

Sloan projected polite interest in what Mellot was saying at
the same time as striving to keep his blood pressure under
control with Crosby. It was not easy.

"I couldn't afford to buy Tom out," said George Mellot,
"and he couldn't afford to get started in business without his
share of the inheritance."

"Yes, I see," said Sloan. It was the classic dilemma. Some
victor or another—he couldn't remember which—had even
imposed laws of inheritance on the vanquished that required
land to be divided equally among all heirs in ever diminish-
ing holdings. Was it called gavelkind? "What did you do?" he
enquired with genuine curiosity.

"Left him as an equal partner in the farm," replied Mellot
concisely, "and went with him as an equal partner in the
business firm."

"Using the farm as surety?" Perhaps the very word firm
derived from farm: perhaps they came of common stock.

"That's right, Inspector."

"Did it work?"

"Our wives got on," said Mellot simply.

That would be the crux of the matter, thought Sloan to himself. Competitive sisters-in-law were the very devil. He said, "So...."

"So until Mellot's Furnishings went public my wife and I owned half of the equity, with Tom and his wife owning the other half."

"And they owned half of the farm?"

"Still do."

"And after the firm went public?"

"We pulled out and just kept a nominal holding for the interest."

Sloan nodded. All that explained the prosperity at Pencombe Farm over and beyond the agricultural.

"Then Ivor Harbeton came along?"

"The big bad wolf," said Mellot tiredly. "We pitched in behind Tom, of course."

"He would have needed all the support he could get," said Sloan. Sometime last night—he couldn't now think when—he had found time to read all about the take-over battle for Mellot's Furnishings.

"Most of the shareholders were behind Tom," said George Mellot. "He's got a businessman's head all right but Harbeton was offering quite a lot."

"Would he have won the day, though, if Harbeton hadn't disappeared when he did?" Sloan leant forward awaiting a reply. This was the question that mattered.

"Your guess is as good as mine, Inspector," said Mellot drily.

Sloan cleared his throat. "Harbeton doesn't seem to be the only person who has disappeared."

Mellot looked up.

"Your brother's not at home," said Sloan. "Martin Ritchie from Stanestede hasn't been seen for a month and a man who has been living rough in Dresham Wood certainly isn't there any more."

The farmer didn't seem interested.

"And someone," added Sloan for good measure, "hit Wendy Lamport over the head last night outside the Lamb and Flag."

Mellot nodded. "We'd heard about that."

"Have you any suggestions to offer?" asked Sloan crisply.

George Mellot shook his head.

"It was your barn," persisted Sloan.

"I know."

"And your fork-lift tractor," he said relentlessly. "Our forensic laboratory have found pieces of skin on the metal."

"Don't!" implored Meg Mellot.

"It was obvious that that would be used," said Mellot without heat. "There is no other way of getting a body up onto the roof. I can see that myself."

"If it had been daytime," persisted Sloan, "you would have heard them. Or the dog would."

"I know," said Mellot tonelessly.

"So you did either see it happen or it must have been while you were both out."

"Yes," agreed Mellot.

"Which?" asked Sloan sharply.

"While we were out," cried Meg Mellot wretchedly. "We didn't see or hear anything, did we, George?"

He shook his head.

"So," continued Sloan inexorably, "you are saying that there was a time when you were both out when it could have happened?"

"Market-day," said Mellot. "We have thought about that. Meg always comes with me to Calleford. Every Thursday without fail."

"And you'd be gone long enough for any amount of mischief, I suppose?"

"Anyone could have got a small army up on the barn roof in the time if they'd had a mind to," said Mellot flatly. "I can't say otherwise."

"When you are away at the market who do you leave here?" asked Sloan although he knew the answer.

"Len Hodge," said George Mellot miserably.

"Them as asks no questions isn't told a lie," said Len Hodge fiercely.

He was standing by the red fire-engine which had come back to its home station in Great Rooden High Street, and was sweating profusely in his thick black uniform. The yellow oilskin trousers of the firemen must have added considerably to their discomfort on a hot day such as this and the other men were changing back into their working clothes as quickly as they could.

Leading fireman Hodge, though, was responsible for seeing that the fire-engine was left ready for its next turn-out.

"Fuel all right, Fred?" he called out over the heads of the two policemen.

"Check," came the muffled reply.

"Hoses?"

"All present and correct."

Detective Inspector Sloan and Detective Constable Crosby had come back into the centre of the village to await the return of the fire-engine. The unmarked police car which had been shadowing the fireman all morning was parked inconspicuously down the road. The two detectives had got a warm reception from Len Hodge.

"Nevertheless," insisted Sloan firmly, "I have a few questions to put to you." He was conscious that he should have made the effort to see Len Hodge last night—except that last night he hadn't suspected that Wendy Lamport was going to come to grief. Last night, too, there had seemed to be plenty of time in which to consider at leisure the implications of a decaying skeleton on a barn roof. Today there hadn't been any time at all.

"And I've got a report to turn in to brigade headquarters," countered the farmworker truculently. The perspiration was streaming down his face. It might have been due to the heavy serge uniform and the increasing heat of the day. On the other hand it might not. "For all that it was a false alarm," he added.

"So have I," responded Sloan with deceptive mildness.

"You haven't got anything on me," said Hodge, tilting his fireman's helmet upwards from his forehead.

"And I," said Sloan evenly, "am not dealing with a false alarm."

Hodge carried on as if the policeman had not spoken. "I'm not having you pinning anything on me neither." He thrust his jaw forward. "I'm not saying nothing, see?"

"What we want to know," continued Sloan in the same low-key tones, "is whether just anyone could have operated that fork-lift tractor at Pencombe."

"Course not," said Len Hodge at once. "Not without knowing how."

"Ah," said Sloan. It was the oldest trick in the book: starting a difficult interview by asking an easy question that anyone could answer.

"It takes time to know how to handle one of them," sniffe
Hodge. "I will say that."

"And a bit of teaching, I daresay," murmured Sloan cun
ningly. Almost nobody could resist an empathetic openin
gambit.

"Just like it does one of these." Len Hodge patted th
majestic Dennis fire-engine. "But when you've learnt ho
it'll do anything for you."

"Such as lift a headless body up onto a roof," said Sloa
sedulously.

Hodge's face darkened again. "If you say so."

"Not me," said Sloan blandly. "It's the forensic scientists a
the Home Office laboratory who say so."

"Same thing," said Hodge immediately.

At the right time and in the right place Sloan would hav
advanced the cause of impartial scientific investigation bein
available to defence and prosecution alike. This, howeve
was neither.

"If," remarked Sloan in a detached way instead, "it ha
been my tractor—"

"Well?"

"And someone else had used it—"

"What about it?"

"Even if they had tried to put it back exactly where I ha
left it—"

Hodge scowled but said nothing intelligible.

"—then," said Sloan, "I think I would have been able t
tell."

"You would, would you?" snarled Hodge. "Well, let me te
you—"

"If it hadn't been me that moved it, that is."

"It wasn't me that—" Hodge stopped and stared a
Sloan.

"No?" said Sloan pleasantly. "I rather thought it wasn't
actually."

"Tricked me, you did, you devil," spluttered Hodge. "
said I wasn't going to say nothing."

"Truth will out," said Crosby sententiously from the side
lines.

"But someone had moved it," said Sloan, undeflected.

"What if they had?" demanded Hodge aggressively. "I
weren't nothing to do with me. It isn't my tractor."

"When?" asked Sloan relentlessly.

"'Bout a month ago," admitted Hodge reluctantly, his eyes down.

"Isn't it kept locked?"

"Not at Pencombe." He shrugged his shoulders. "There's nobody about much as a rule. Besides, it's always on the go."

"This time—"

"I park it in the barn," explained Hodge. "It just fits into a space there if you're careful. Between an old harrow and the grain-drier. There's exactly enough room for it."

Sloan nodded encouragingly. Verisimilitude was the name of what he was looking for.

"Whoever put it back wasn't careful, that's all," said Hodge flatly. "They caught the harrow with one of the forks. It wasn't me. I've never done that."

"When?" Sloan would send someone to check on the harrow as soon as he could. "Night-time or day-time?"

"Search me." He turned back to the fire-engine. "It was an afternoon when I noticed it, but that doesn't mean anything."

"Did you mention it to anyone else at the time?"

"Nope." He shook his head. "It's not my place to mention it. It's none of my business if my governor bashes a bit of his own property."

"Which governor, Hodge?" asked Sloan softly.

All the bounce left the man. He went down like a pricked balloon, his shoulders sagging suddenly. "You know about Tom, then, do you?"

"We do," said Sloan. He had been reared in the good old professional school of interrogation where there was no nonsense about not hitting a man when he was down. It was easier, for one thing. He didn't hesitate to press home his advantage, either, by adding ominously, "All about him."

"Well, then . . ." Hodge turned away.

"Except where he is at the moment," said Sloan truthfully. That, he reminded himself, went for the man in the wood, too, and for Martin Ritchie. They hadn't exactly made a lot of progress to date in police terms.

"Not a man to stand still is Tom," observed Hodge, clambering up into the driver's seat of the fire-engine. "I've got to put this away now. Mind your backs. . . ."

Sloan stepped aside. Minding your back was an old army saying. It was easier said than done in the police force. So was standing still. They had another saying in the army that

didn't do for the police at all. "Right or wrong, stand still."
What went down well in the parade-ground—make a mistake
there and ten to one it wouldn't be noticed if you stood still:
move and it would—wouldn't do you any good at all in the
constabulary. Standing still would be viewed by the director
of public prosecutions as culpable and mistakes had very little
chance of not being noticed in the sort of scrutiny applied by
the likes of Superintendent Leeyes.

"Wendy Lamport's pretty bad," said Sloan, raising his
voice as the engine was started up by Hodge. Even thinking
about Superintendent Leeyes en passant kept a man's mind
on the job.

If Hodge made a reply to this it was drowned by the noise
of the powerful Dennis engine. Sloan waited until it had been
driven out of the fire station and positioned ready for its next
call-out. Hodge climbed down again and carefully placed the
door in an open position. Seconds could count at a fire.

"I said Wendy Lamport's pretty bad," repeated Sloan
firmly. He knew exactly where Wendy Lamport was at this
moment and it didn't help one little bit.

"I heard you." Hodge jerked his head. "I didn't hit her, if
that's what you wanted to know."

"But do you know who did?" asked Sloan directly.

"No, I don't."

"The man in Dresham Wood?" hazarded Sloan.

The farmworker's response to this was completely unexpected. To Sloan's utter surprise Len Hodge's face split into a
broad grin that extended from ear to ear. "Him?" he laughed.
"That's good, that is."

"What do you mean?"

"Him?" he said richly. "He wouldn't hurt a fly." Hodge
started to walk toward his own car and then paused and said
over his shoulder, "That's his whole trouble."

"Just a minute, Hodge—"

It was no good. Len Hodge had driven off.

The unmarked police car which had been shadowing him
all morning waited a few moments and then drove off
unobtrusively after him.

The radio of their police car was chattering away as Detective Inspector Sloan and Detective Constable Crosby got
back to it. Crosby fiddled with the direction tuner and then
bent forward attentively, listening hard.

"Ted Mason's found something that might have been used to take the head off, sir," he announced, straightening up again.

Sloan nodded morosely. "It had to be around somewhere."

"In the barn at Lowercombe," said Crosby.

"I heard," growled Sloan. He had just had a major suspect laughed out of court and wasn't very pleased about it.

"A sugar-beet cutter."

"I see." He wondered what Dr. Buck Ruxton had used to cut up his wife.

"It's gone to Forensic."

"What we want now," declared Sloan with feeling, "is a Peterkin."

"Pardon, sir?"

"He found something large and smooth and round."

"Did he, sir?"

"And showed it to little Wilhelmine."

"Well, I never."

"They both took it to Old Kaspar."

Crosby kept a prudent silence at this.

"At Blenheim."

Crosby looked distinctly uneasy now.

" 'Twas a famous victory," said Sloan sourly.

"Was it, sir?"

"This isn't going to be, Crosby."

"No, sir." Crosby switched off the engine.

"This is going to be a disaster," forecast Sloan. He had never thought for one moment that the notion that the man in the wood might be a murderer would be something that Len Hodge would find risible. The funny thing was the fact that it exonerated him more quickly than any amount of explanation.

"Where to, sir?" enquired the constable practically.

"I don't think it really matters."

"Pencombe?"

"Cold Comfort Farm, more like."

"Headquarters?"

"Perish the thought, Crosby." There would be scant comfort at Berebury Police Station, either. And at the very least the press would be there, clamouring for tidbits that he couldn't—wouldn't, anyway—give them. To say nothing of Superintendent Leeyes wanting to know why he hadn't made an arrest—any arrest—yet.

The detective constable pointed along the High Street to the village inn. "The Lamb and Flag?"

Sloan regarded the public house with disfavour. There was something seriously wrong with the anatomy of the lamb on the signboard but he hadn't time to examine it more closely. "Nobody knows anything there and if they do, they aren't going to tell us." To the best of Sloan's knowledge and belief the Lamb and Flag had been wrung dry of facts as soon as Wendy Lamport had been found. He turned his gaze back to the fire station. Did Len Hodge's laughter really let out the man in the wood? On the whole Sloan thought so. It had been so spontaneous.

"Sir," said Crosby, "have you heard the one about the skeleton?"

"What's that?" He brought his mind back to the police car with an effort.

"The one about why the skeleton didn't go to the ball."

"No," responded Sloan heatedly, "and I—"

"Because he had nobody to go with. Get it?" asked Crosby. "No body."

"I get it." Sloan's ire subsided as quickly as it had risen. If soldiers sought reputation in the cannon's mouth there was no reason why detective constables shouldn't crack a bad joke or two in a murder enquiry when there wasn't anything more constructive to do.

The trouble with this case was that all they had was the ingredients without knowing what the recipe was for. At hand, so to speak, were a naked headless corpse, a weapon and an injured girl. Missing with varying degrees of relevance— but undoubtedly germane—were a defaulting financier, an absconding husband and—

The police radio came to life again.

Crosby answered with their call sign and then listened with his notepad at the ready. "The fingerprints on the bottles in the wood—"

"Yes?" At this moment Sloan didn't have a harsh word to say about computers or the Criminal Record Office.

"Known."

Sloan perked up. They weren't totally in Indian country, then.

"Luke Michael Bailey," repeated Crosby aloud, writing fast. "Numerous convictions all over the country for offences associated with alcohol abuse."

"Ah . . ." Sloan sank back in the passenger seat.
"Last known address—"
"Yes?" said Sloan.
"A drying-out centre for alcoholics in Luston."

EIGHTEEN

•

Depart in peace

The engine of the police car was still running.

"Back to Lowercombe, then, sir?" asked Crosby.

"Back to the drawing-board, if you ask me," responded Sloan mordantly. In his experience alcoholics didn't as a rule commit murder except by accident in a drunken brawl. And every alcoholic he had ever known lacked the resolution to conceal dead and dismembered bodies in carefully thought-out hiding places.

"It's Sam Bailey's son for sure," pronounced Crosby. He wrinkled his brow. "Now I come to think about it, Mrs. Ritchie did mention that Sam had a son."

Sloan nodded. "And he called his wife 'Mother,' didn't he?" There had been a prodigal son in the offing in Great Rooden all right but it had been somewhere else. It wasn't at Pencombe Farm with the Mellots, then, where there had been a definite return of the native but at Lowercombe with the Baileys. . . .

"His mother will have been feeding him, won't she?" said Crosby. "With what was left over from the table, I expect."

"Better than the husks that the swine did eat," said Sloan biblically. "Fed, forgiven and known again" was how Kipling had put it.

"Except that alcoholics don't get hungry anyway," offered Crosby out of his own experience on the beat. The railway arches at Berebury provided shelter of a sort for them and had to be visited by foot constables on night duty.

"Sam Bailey won't have known about him—Luke, did you say the name was?—being there in the wood," said Sloan confidently. Sanctuary Wood—no, that had been somewhere else. "He's not the sort of man to kill a fatted calf is Sam Bailey."

"At least," said Crosby, "we know now how Mrs. Bailey got the leaf-mould on her shoes. That's something."

"Len Hodge knew about him being there in the wood," said Sloan thoughtfully. "That's why the first thing he did when he heard about the finger was to go over there. Do you remember?"

"To check."

"And Mrs. Bailey was pretty agitated, too, at first," recollected Sloan. "Until we told her it was an old finger, and then she calmed down. I reckon she took off with Luke until the search of the wood was over."

"If," said Crosby, his face contorted with thought, "Len Hodge needed to check that the body wasn't Luke Bailey's, doesn't that mean that he didn't know whose it really was?"

"Well done," applauded Sloan softly. "Go on."

The constable continued much more tentatively. "The body could still have been Ivor Harbeton's and Len Hodge not have known about it, I suppose?"

"At first," said Sloan.

"Put there by one Mellot—"

"Or the other."

"Or both."

"It could," agreed Sloan.

"But Hodge did know about the fork-lift tractor having been moved while he wasn't there, didn't he? All along."

"He will have known," said Sloan patiently, "but I daresay the fact only became really significant after the body was found and Hodge put two and two together." The assistant chief constable, who was a great man for Latin tags, had a favourite one for events that followed on: *post hoc ergo propter hoc*.

"That's when Hodge realised it could have been one of the Mellots who had done the dastardly deed," deduced Crosby, "and clammed up."

"I think so," said Sloan slowly. As well as having the wrong Prodigal Son in mind he'd probably got the wrong school tie, too. Tom and George Mellot and Len Hodge would have known each other all their early lives—as well as Luke Bailey. You didn't shop your childhood companions. Nor your employer if it came to that—not if you were old-fashioned, that is.

"Finding out it was Luke Bailey in the wood then," concluded Crosby with rustic simplicity, "is a snake and not a ladder."

"A snare and a delusion," agreed Sloan gravely.

Superintendent Leeyes wouldn't have chosen either metaphor but his sentiment woud have been the same.

"So we've got to begin at the beginning again." Crosby leant forward and switched off the engine.

"Except," said Sloan appositely, "that we don't even know when that was." In this game you actually had to find square one first before you could get back to it. . . .

"A finger on a footpath," said Crosby.

Sloan shook his head. "That came later. The finger being found on the footpath was just bad luck on the murderer's part."

"You can't win them all," said Crosby ambiguously.

"The finger was just where we came in," said Sloan. Fate had thrown a six for them to start.

"But—" Crosby started to say something.

"It all began at least a month before that," said Sloan firmly.

"But what did it begin with?" asked the constable.

Sloan shrugged his shoulders. Where did murder begin? Some would say with Cain and Abel. Some—the Freudians— would say with Adam and Eve. And as for what with—that was anybody's guess in this particular case. Greed, jealousy, revenge, lust . . . A judge would instruct a jury that the motive was irrelevant—the crime was what counted and the crime was what should be punished—but motive mattered to an investigating officer all right. It usually mattered to a jury as well despite what the judge said.

"I reckon George Mellot thinks it was Tom Mellot, too," offered Crosby after a moment. "If it wasn't himself, that is."

"Not so much brother against brother as brother protecting brother," agreed Sloan tacitly.

"With George giving Tom a helping hand," added Crosby for good measure, "if he needed it."

"Maybe, maybe not." Sloan wasn't sure.

"And Len Hodge pitching in too, for that matter."

"That would figure, all right."

"And Tom decamps when he gets the word from brother George that all is up."

"That fits too." Sloan nodded. "So does Mrs. Meg Mellot fainting at the mention of Ivor Harbeton's name."

"The body was got up there without being noticed, remember," said Crosby, "or the dog barking. The Mellots could have put it up there any time they liked."

"Either of them."

"Both of them."

"There was just one other time when someone else could have done that, too," said Sloan fairly. There was a word space navigators and oil-rig engineers used for a short period of time when circumstances were favourable to an enterprise. They got it from the weathermen. "There was a window—"

"Pardon, sir?"

"Market-day," said Sloan without explanation. "George and Meg Mellot always went into Calleford on market-day. Everyone knew that."

"Hodge would have been there, though," objected Crosby.

"Hodge might have been got out of the way."

"How?"

Sloan looked along the High Street and pointed in the direction of the fire-engine. The idea had just come to him. "False alarm, malicious intent," he said. "He'd have answered a fire-alarm."

Superintendent Leeyes was at his most peppery. He regarded his opposite number in the Calleshire Fire Brigade as a necesary evil and didn't want to be beholden to him for anything. Firemen were useful for extinguishing fires and their heavy lifting gear certainly came in handy on occasion, but in his view they ranked well below the constabulary as a public service. From time to time at the golf-club he played a needle match with the chief fire officer at Berebury which was very trying for all concerned as the fireman was the better player. Superintendent Leeyes attributed this to the more flexible shift system enjoyed by the fire service. The feeling at the police station was that he would have shot at a sitting bird, too, if he could.

"It would have been theoretically possible for that body to have been hauled up onto that roof in broad daylight on market-day if Len Hodge wasn't there, Sloan," he barked. "Is that what you're trying to say?"

"Yes, sir. He coughed. "We know—and so presumably do a great many people—that George and Meg Mellot go into Calleford together every Thursday."

"Leaving Len Hodge at Pencombe?"

"And the dog," said Sloan down the telephone.

"Well?"

"Len Hodge is a leading fireman with the Great Rooden retained brigade."

"I get you." He grunted. "And you want to know if they had a call-out on the first Thursday in June?"

"Any Thursday," replied Sloan. "The body could have been

hidden until the Thursday of the week after." The forensic scientists were not prepared to be definite to within days about how long it had been on the roof.

"The head," said Leeyes pointedly, "has been hidden without being found."

"We've got the instrument that took it off," said Sloan. His superior officer had a positive gift for putting a man on the defensive.

"No fingerprints on it, though," he said.

"No," said Sloan. That would have been too much to hope for. Besides, they were not dealing with a fool. Or fools.

"What was it?"

"A tool for topping sugar-beet."

"Did you know, Sloan, that stage beheading is done with a cabbage?"

"No, sir." There were a lot of things he did not know. He cleared his throat. "We're on the track of the man in the wood." He explained about Luke Bailey.

"Proper biblical touch, eh, Sloan?"

"Yes, sir," he said, his memory teasing him. Somewhere in the Bible there had been something closer to the case than the parable of the Prodigal Son but he couldn't for the life of him bring it to mind.

"That's who Hodge will have been fighting with in the pub, I suppose?"

"So it will." Sloan hadn't got round to thinking about that.

"Didn't want him showing up there, of course. Give the game away."

"Not when he was supposed to be lying low in the wood," he agreed.

"Where does all this leave you, Sloan?"

"Not very much further forward, sir, I'm afraid."

"Find out who it was up there on the roof," adjured Leeyes for the second time, "and you'll be nearer to knowing who did it."

"Chance would be a fine thing," rejoined Sloan.

"What was that?" The line crackled.

"Nothing, sir."

"Where do you go from here?"

"I don't know," said Sloan truthfully.

Detective Inspector Sloan walked back from the telephone-box to the police car. Some calls were too private for the police radio. People talked about the freedom of the air. That meant that the air was free to everybody and there were those who could pick up the waveband that the constabulary used.

Crosby looked up as he approached.

"The Great Rooden retained fire brigade," announced Sloan, not without a little pardonable portentousness, "answered a three-nines call on Thursday, June first, at ten hundred hours to the village of Cullingoak."

"Did they, sir?"

"Which is at the absolute edge of the area they cover."

"Surprise, surprise."

"To a fictitious address," added Sloan, although the lily didn't need gilding.

"False alarm, malicious intent," spelled out Crosby, "to get Hodge out of the way."

"They did not report back to their home station until nearly eleven o'clock that morning."

"It wouldn't take long to start up that fork-lift tractor, run it up to gutter level and tip the body out," said Crosby helpfully.

"And the dog could bark as much as it liked," said Sloan. It wasn't going to be like a certain Sherlock Holmes story after all. That was a relief. Art imitating life was one thing. Life imitating literature was quite another.

"With only the murderer to hear," said Crosby.

"Or murderers." They still didn't even know yet how many persons there were with blood on their hands. There was altogether too much that they did not know in this case. "We may not know who," added Sloan grimly, "but at least we are beginning to know how and when."

Crosby scratched his head. "I suppose Len Hodge might have only been got out of the way to give him an alibi."

"We might make a detective out of you yet, Crosby," said Sloan warmly. Being a good investigating officer called for a certain quality of mind which took nothing for granted.

Crosby squinted modestly at his toes and said, "Hodge could have put the body up there then answered a fire call and then damaged the tractor afterwards on purpose."

"Nothing to stop him," agreed Sloan. Len Hodge couldn't be said to be in the clear yet by any manner of means: but nevertheless there had been a time when the farmyard at Pencombe had been deserted for long enough for a body to be hidden. . . .

"Doesn't get us very far, sir, does it?" said Crosby gloomily.

"No," said Sloan. Blind alleys were something a police officer had to get used to. Unsolved cases, too, had to be lived with as well as lived down. He sighed. "We'd better get going, I suppose."

Crosby leaned forward to switch on the engine once more. "Where to, sir?"

"Back to base," he said unwillingly. There would be no comfort to be had at the police station. Worse, there might be a message from the hospital about Wendy Lamport. "There's something else we haven't thought about, Crosby."

"Sir?"

"If Luke Bailey isn't involved with the body," said Sloan, "why did Wendy Lamport get clobbered last night just because she talked about the wood?"

"Search me," said Crosby, engaging gear.

"What happened to her wasn't an accident," said Sloan with asperity. "That at least was a certain thing in an uncertain world."

The detective constable steered the police car away from the kerb. "No."

"The murderer must have been around, mustn't he? To have hit her, I mean." Anything else would smack too much of coincidence.

"Yes, sir." They were level with the Great Rooden Fire Station now.

"He did that all right, sir." Their vehicle drew level with the Lamb and Flag car-park next. Wendy Lamport's little car was still standing there. Orange ribbons marked out the area the forensic people had gone over.

Sloan stared into the pub car-park as they went by. It was funny how they all automatically fell into the way of thinking of all murderers as men, but as the lawyers said the male embraced the female. He had an idea that the one he had been thinking about in the Bible had been female. There was a parallel somewhere that he couldn't pin down. Perhaps it would come to him if he thought about something else.

"Remind me of all who were there last night," he said.

"Len Hodge," said Crosby.

They had exhausted the subject of Len Hodge.

"Paul Hucham."

"All we know about him," said Sloan realistically, "is that he can lift a sheep. I saw him doing it."

"So, presumably, can George Mellot," said Crosby.

"To say nothing of his brother Tom," said Sloan. "He's younger, too."

"And Luke Bailey," added Crosby. "He could have been in the car-park without anyone being the wiser. Drunks have a lot of strength." This was something else he'd learnt early on the beat.

"Spoilt for choice," said Sloan sourly. "That's our trouble. At least I don't see Mrs. Ritchie lifting a sheep. Or anything else for that matter."

Crosby nodded. "Nor driving a fork-lift tractor. She doesn't even look the part."

"All the same, I must say it would have been a help to have had that note she threw on the fire." People like Martin Ritchie could always disappear if they put their minds to it. The insurance companies knew that.

"What fire?"

"The kitchen fire," said Sloan absently. There had been several famous cases of disappearance. Usually there was a seven-year wait for inheritance, but at least Andrina Ritchie could carry on as a full partner with the farm.

"There wasn't a fire in the kitchen," said Crosby.

Sloan stiffened. "Say that again."

"There wasn't a fire in the kitchen," repeated the constable obediently.

Sloan stared at him. "Are you sure?"

"Dead certain," insisted the constable, aggrieved. "It was all electric. Everything. Not like Pencombe. There wasn't a real fire anywhere."

"Of course! I remember now," said Sloan softly. "The stream gives them all the power they need for free at Stanestede." Paul Hucham had told him that, hadn't he?

When they had been up on the hill near the path from Uppercombe down to Stanestede.

"They have their own generator or something," said Crosby. "She said so."

"I do believe," breathed Sloan, thinking furiously, "that that might be the lie circumstantial."

"Beg pardon, sir?"

"Something Touchstone said," replied Sloan. William Shakespeare had struck the right note as usual.

"Who's Touchstone?" asked Crosby.

"A clown," said Sloan crisply. "Crosby, your notebook."

"Here, sir."

"Let me see exactly what Andrina Ritchie said to you when you went to Stanestede."

"Nothing very important, sir. I told you at the time."

Sloan turned the pages back until he found the transcript. He studied it for a full minute and then said, "You were wrong about that, Crosby."

"Me, sir?"

"You, Crosby." There was an old tune that went, "It's not what you say, it's the way that you say it." That went for what Andrina Ritchie had said to Crosby, too. "Read it again."

"Yes, sir."

"We're not going back to Berebury."

"No, sir?"

"Take the next right turn," he commanded.

"Yes, sir."

"And you can put your foot down."

"Thank you, sir," said Crosby joyously.

"I've got one or two questions to ask Mrs. Andrina Ritchie."

"Stone the crows," said Detective Constable Crosby as he accelerated.

"Let's look to the lady," said Sloan more aptly still.

"Sloan," thundered Superintendent Leeyes down the telephone, "are you out of your mind?"

"No, sir."

"What has someone in the Bible called Judith got to do with your arresting Andrina Ritchie?"

"Not the Bible exactly, sir. The Apocrypha."

It was immediately apparent that to the superintendent they were one and the same. He growled dangerously.

"Judith," explained Sloan hastily, "cut off Holofernes's head while he was in bed beside her. For the good of her country."

"Thinking of England, was she?"

"Israel, actually." He coughed. "I suppose you might call her an early female activist."

"Sloan, do I have to come to Great Rooden myself to get any sense out of you?"

"No, sir," he said hurriedly. "I'll explain. We hadn't thought a lot about Andrina Ritchie because we didn't see her humping a headless body down to Pencombe." In the Apocrypha Judith had carried off Holofernes's head in a basket and left the body behind.

"Somebody did."

"Paul Hucham," said Sloan. "He put it on the roof."

"Ah . . ." Leeyes let out a sigh. "An eternal triangle."

"I'm afraid so, sir," agreed Sloan. "No one suspected anything because they weren't seen together. There was no need for anyone to see them because there was a path between the two farms and anyway it's all very remote up there on the hill."

Leeyes grunted. "The old, old story . . ."

"They were very clever."

"Nearly pulled it off, did they?" That was the police yardstick of a villain's cunning.

"They were very unlucky," said Sloan temperately. "The body might not have been found up on that roof for years. I don't suppose we'll ever find the head. And without a head and therefore without teeth, when it was found it might not have ever been identified."

"Especially with a cold trail," said Leeyes realistically.

"Exactly, sir." He cleared his throat. "But for that crow dropping the finger and Wendy Lamport finding it they would have got away with murder."

"She's come round, by the way," said Leeyes. "Doesn't remember a thing after bending down to put the car key in the lock."

"That will have been Hucham," said Sloan. "He was in the Lamb and Flag, too. I reckon he saw an opportunity to confuse the issue and took it. In every respect this murder was a very carefully planned affair." He paused to marshal his own thoughts. "I think it may well have been the decamping of Ivor Harbeton that gave them the idea."

"Everyone knew about that," said Leeyes.

"And Paul Hucham and Andrina Ritchie also knew of the link between George Mellot and Mellot's Furnishings," said Sloan. "I reckon they decided to take advantage of it."

"So that if there were any suspicion it fell on the Mellots?"

"Yes, sir. They had to take a chance on the heights being similar, of course, but they didn't reckon on the body being found anyway."

"Clever," mused Leeyes.

"Cold-blooded," said Sloan. "I reckon they left Martin Ritchie's car at the market during the night. I don't know where Harbeton decamped to or where Tom Mellot and his wife have gone, but—"

"Neither do I," interrupted Leeyes, "but there's a white Sealyham answering to our description in a kennel at Dover."

"A few days in France," concluded Sloan. He wasn't interested in Tom Mellot any more. He went back to Mrs. Ritchie. "There wasn't any real reason for the woman to report her husband as missing either," said Sloan.

"Hucham rang the solicitor for her, I suppose?"

"He only spoke to the secretary," Sloan reminded him. "He rang at a time when he knew Mr. Puckle would be in court."

Leeyes said, "Husbands do take off."

"We ran the usual checks for him," said Sloan, "but I must say a girl called Beverley had a convincing ring to it. So," he added ruefully, "did Andrina Ritchie's attitude."

"Nearly fooled you, did she, Sloan?"

"Truth will out," said Sloan sedately. "It emerged when she was talking to Crosby. I've just checked."

"To Crosby?" echoed Leeyes. "I don't believe it."

"She consistently referred to her husband in the past tense all the way through the interview. It's very difficult not to, sir, if you know that someone is dead. Your subconscious takes over."

"The court doesn't like psychological stuff," said Leeyes.

"They'll like the blood-stains on the carpet," said Sloan comfortably. "I reckon she had a rubber sheet on the mattress but the carpet got splashed. Crosby's working on it now."

Sloan went back to Crosby in the bedroom. "I should have got the answer a long time ago." Mrs. Andrina Coonie Ritchie had been taken away tight-lipped and talking only about lawyers.

The constable was more philosophical. "Bit of a turn-up for the book, a woman."

"The devil is an Equal Opportunities Employer," said Sloan. At least Judith had had the good of Israel at heart when she murdered Holofernes. Andrina Ritchie had been thinking only of Andrina Ritchie.

"Now I come to think of it," said Crosby, who was on his hands and knees on the floor, "she was the one who told us about Sam Bailey having a no-good boyo for a son, too."

"It was all very well thought out, Crosby. No doubt about that." He had sent Constable Mason up the hill to arrest Paul Hucham. He hoped he hadn't forgotten how to do it. Complicity was the word he would use when he charged Hucham. The leadership lay with the lady: the mode of death demonstrated that.

"That'll be why she used the Baileys' beet-topper," said Crosby, shifting his knee.

"I should have got there a long time ago," said Sloan. How had the rest of that old ballad about the twa corbies and the new-slain knight gone?

> His hound is to the hunting gane,
> His hawk to fetch the wild-fowl hame
> His lady's ta'en anither mate . . .

Detective Constable Crosby's contribution came in verse form, too. But parody. He straightened his back and chanted, "Red stains on the carpet, red stains on the knife, Poor old fellow, cut up by your wife."

The tune was "Red Sails in the Sunset": the sentiment quite sincere.

"Morning, Seedy." Inspector Harpe from Traffic Division bumped into Sloan in the corridor of the police station just after he got back there.

"Morning, Harry." Sloan looked at his watch. It was still only Monday morning.

"Quiet weekend?"

"Not really," replied Sloan, adding politely, "And you?"

"Two pile-ups and seven under the influence," said the traffic man.

"Ah."

"And then I come in to this." Happy Harry waved a letter in his hand.

"What is it?"

"From the Calleshire Ornithological Society."

"Take my advice, Harry. If it's anything to do with crows give it a miss."

"Crows?" said Harpe blankly. "It's not crows they're on about. It's kestrels. Seems that kestrels have discovered that their prey can't cross motorways—dormice and the like—"

"Well, well."

"So they drive 'em up to the edge of the road and then catch them—using the motorway as a trap."

"Better than using it as a race-track."

"What— Oh, yes, of course." He looked at the letter again.

"These bird people want to be allowed on the motorway to study the kestrels. . . ."

Detective Inspector Sloan had a very long report to write. "I should send the Flying Squad if I were you. . . ."

ABOUT THE AUTHOR

CATHERINE AIRD had never tried her hand at writing suspense stories before publishing *The Religious Body*—a novel which immediately established her as one of the genre's most talented writers. *A Late Phoenix, The Stately Home Murder, His Burial Too, Some Die Eloquent, Henrietta Who?* and *A Most Contagious Game* have subsequently enhanced her reputation. Her ancestry is Scottish, but she now lives in a village in East Kent, near Canterbury, where she serves as an aide to her father, a doctor, and takes an interest in local affairs.

Masters
of
Mystery

With these new mystery titles, Bantam takes you to the scene of the crime. These masters of mystery follow in the tradition of the Great British and American crime writers. You'll meet all these talented sleuths as they get to the bottom of even the most baffling crimes.